"But you seem glad for *everything!*"

Pollyanna laughed. "Well, that's the game, you know."

"The *game?*"

"Yes. The 'Just Being Glad' game. . . . The game was to find something about everything to be glad for—no ⸱r what it was," explained Pollyanna "So we began playing right ᵇᵉ crutches."

ᵇ⸱ see anything to be glad ι pair of crutches when ⸱⸱ ᵉd ι ⸱⸱l!"

Pollyanna clapped her hands in delight. "But there is! There is! Of course, couldn't see it at first, either, Nancy. Father had to explain it to me."

"Then I guess you'll have to tell me, too," Nancy said.

"Why, just be glad because *you don't need them!*" Pollyanna shouted, triumphantly. "You see. It's really easy— once you know how!"

A Background Note about *Pollyanna*

Pollyanna takes place in the early 1910s. At that time, missionary ministers moved out West, hoping to spread their religious beliefs along the American frontier. Churches sometimes sent them books, clothing, and other supplies in "missionary barrels." Life was hard for these missionary families, who were paid little and who often lived far from schools, stores, and hospitals.

During the 1910s, some women form organizations called Ladies' Aid Societies. T groups gave women a place to socialize money for their churches, and do charity w the poor.

At this time, most people still traveled b or horse-drawn carriages. But cars were gr starting to take over the roads—startling horses and pedestrians with their speed and po

1913 was a time when the world was chang rapidly—and when Pollyanna was rapidly changi her world.

ELEANOR H. PORTER

Pollyanna

Edited, and with an Afterword,
by Lisa Barsky

TP THE TOWNSEND LIBRARY

POLLYANNA

TP THE TOWNSEND LIBRARY

For more titles in the Townsend Library,
visit our website: www.townsendpress.com

All new material in this edition is
copyright © 2009 by Townsend Press.
Printed in the United States of America

0 9 8 7 6 5 4 3 2 1

Illustrations copyright © 2009 by Hal Taylor

Townsend Press, Inc.
439 Kelley Drive
West Berlin, NJ 08091
cs@townsendpress.com

ISBN-13: 978-1-59194-112-5
ISBN-10: 1-59194-112-1

Library of Congress Control Number:
2008922269

Contents

Afterword

Chapter 1

Miss Polly

Miss Polly Harrington hurried into her kitchen this June morning. She didn't usually move so quickly. In fact, she took pride in being a calm person. But today she was actually hurrying.

Nancy looked up from washing the dishes. She'd been working in Miss Polly's kitchen for only two months. But she already knew that her employer never hurried.

"Nancy!"

"Yes, ma'am," Nancy answered, as she kept drying the pitcher in her hand.

"Nancy," Miss Polly commanded. "When I talk to you, I want you to stop what you're doing and listen to me."

Nancy's face darkened. She was so upset at being scolded that she almost dropped the pitcher. "Yes, ma'am. I will, ma'am," she stammered. "I kept doing my work because earlier you told me to hurry up with the dishes."

Miss Polly frowned.

"That will do, Nancy. I did not ask for explanations. I asked for your *attention*."

"Yes, ma'am," Nancy sighed. Would she ever be able to please this woman?

This was Nancy's first real job. Her father had died recently, and she needed to help support her sick mother and her three younger sisters. At first Nancy was pleased to work in this large house up on the hill. She'd always known that Miss Polly Harrington was one of the richest people in town. But now she also knew that Miss Polly was a stern woman who always wore a severe expression on her face. She frowned if a door banged or if a knife made noise when it fell on the floor. And she never smiled—even when the doors and the knives were quiet.

Now Miss Polly gave her more orders. "When you've finished your morning work, you may clear out of the little attic room at the top of the stairs. Then make up the cot bed. And of course, sweep and clean the room."

"Yes, ma'am."

Miss Polly hesitated. Then she said, "I suppose I may as well tell you now, Nancy. My niece, Miss Pollyanna Whittier, is coming to live with me and will sleep in that room. She is eleven years old."

"A little girl coming here, Miss Harrington? Oh, won't that be nice!" exclaimed Nancy. She was thinking how her own little sisters brought sunshine to their home.

"Nice? Well, that isn't exactly the word I would use," Miss Polly answered stiffly. "However, I intend to make the best of it. I'd like to think that I'm a good woman. And I know my duty."

Nancy's face darkened again. "Of course, ma'am. I just thought that a little girl might . . ." She hesitated. "Well, she might brighten things up for you."

"Thank you," Miss Polly answered dryly. "However, I see no need for that."

Thinking that this lonely little stranger should be welcomed into her new home, Nancy suggested, "But of course you—you'd want to have her, your sister's child."

"Well, really, Nancy," Miss Polly replied, looking down her nose. "Just because my sister was silly enough to get married and bring one more unnecessary child into this crowded world— well, I can't see why I'd particularly want to take care of her myself. However, as I said before, I know my duty. See that you clean the corners, Nancy," she finished sharply, leaving the room.

"Yes, ma'am," sighed Nancy, picking up the half-dried pitcher.

Miss Polly went into her room and looked again at the letter she had received two days ago. It had come to her home in Beldingsville, Vermont, all the way from a remote town out West. And it had come as an unpleasant surprise.

Dear Madam:

I regret to inform you that the Reverend John Whittier died two weeks ago, leaving one child, an eleven-year-old girl. He left almost nothing else except a few books. As you know, he earned very little money as the pastor of our small mission church.

I understand that he married your sister, who died some time ago, and that you did not get along well with him. But he thought that for your sister's sake you might want to bring up the child among her own relatives in the East.

Please let us know right away if you can take her. A man and woman from here can travel with Pollyanna as far as Boston. There they can put her on a train to Beldingsville.

Respectfully yours,
Jeremiah O. White

With a frown, Miss Polly put away the letter. She'd written back yesterday, saying, of course, that she would take the child. It would be an unpleasant task, but she knew her duty.

Miss Polly remembered when one of her two older sisters, Jennie, was only twenty years old. Her family wanted Jennie to marry a wealthy, older man. But she refused. Against her family's wishes,

Jennie insisted on marrying a young minister, who was full of youthful ideals and enthusiasm. So she went out West with him, to become a missionary's wife.

After that, the family had nothing more to do with her. Jennie continued to write for a while. In her last letter, she wrote that she had named her baby "Pollyanna" in honor of her two sisters, Polly and Anna. But a few years later a note arrived from a little town out West. In it, her heart-broken husband told them of Jennie's death.

Miss Polly then thought about all the changes that the past twenty-five hears had brought to her own life. She was forty now, and completely alone in the world. Father, mother, sisters—all were dead. For years, she had been living on the money her father left her. And there she lived—alone in the large house. Some people pitied her lonely life and encouraged her to have someone live with her. But Miss Polly wanted neither their sympathy nor their advice. She said she was not lonely. She liked being by herself. She preferred quiet. But now—

Miss Polly frowned, her lips tightly shut. She was glad, of course, that she was a good woman. She knew her duty, and she was strong enough to do it. But "Pollyanna"! What a ridiculous name!

Chapter
2

Old Tom and Nancy

In the little attic room, Nancy swept and scrubbed hard. She made sure that she cleaned the corners especially well. Nancy was afraid to disobey her employer. But her angry jabs at the dirt showed her true feelings. "I just wish I could dig out the corners of her *soul*!" Nancy muttered. "Now *that* could sure use some cleaning! How can she stick that blessed child 'way off up here in this hot little room. In the winter, it's not even heated! And with all the rooms in this big house to pick and choose from! 'Unnecessary' children, indeed! Humph!" snapped Nancy, wringing her rag so hard her fingers ached. "It's not *children* that are unnecessary!"

When she'd finished her task, Nancy looked around the bare little room in disgust. "Well, my part's done," she sighed. "There's no dirt here anymore—but there's mighty little else, either. Poor

little soul! A fine place to put a homesick, lonely child!"

As she left, she closed the door with a bang. "Oh, dear!" she exclaimed. But then she said stubbornly, "Well, I don't care. I hope she *did* hear the bang!"

In the garden later that afternoon, Nancy stopped to speak with Old Tom. He'd been pulling weeds and shoveling paths on the Harrington property for many years.

"Mr. Tom," Nancy began, checking to make sure that no one could see her. "Did you know that a little girl was coming to live here with Miss Polly?"

"A *what?*" the old man asked, straightening his bent back with difficulty.

"A little girl."

"Aw, you're just joking," Tom answered. "Next you'll try to tell me that the sun's going to set in the *east*!"

"But it's the truth. Miss Polly told me so herself. It's her eleven-year-old niece."

The man's jaw dropped. Then a tender light came into his faded eyes. "Why, it can't be—but it must be—Miss Jennie's little girl! And to think I've lived to see it!"

"Who was Miss Jennie?" Nancy asked.

"She was Mr. and Mrs. Harrington's oldest daughter. And she was an angel! She was twenty when she married and went away. I heard that all her babies died except the last one. That must be the one that's coming."

"And she's going to have to sleep in the *attic*. Shame on *her*!" Nancy muttered.

Old Tom frowned. But then he grinned and said, "I wonder what Miss Polly will do with a child in the house."

"Humph!" snapped Nancy. "I wonder what a child will do with *Miss Polly* in the house!"

The old man laughed. "I'm afraid you don't like Miss Polly very much."

Nancy snarled, "As if *anybody* could ever like her!"

"I guess maybe you didn't know about Miss Polly's love affair," Tom said quietly.

"Love affair? Not likely. Not *her*!"

"Oh yes. And the fellow's still living right here in this town!"

"Who is he?"

"Oh, I can't tell you that. It wouldn't be right." The old man was still loyal to the family he had served and loved for so long.

"But it just doesn't seem possible—*her* and a lover!"

Old Tom shook his head. "You didn't know Miss Polly the way I did. She used to be so beautiful. And she would be now, if she'd just let herself be."

"Beautiful? *Miss Polly?*"

"Why yes. If only she'd just loosen her hair and let it fall gracefully, like she used to. And wear lacey dresses and all. You'd see how beautiful she is. You know, Miss Polly isn't old, Nancy."

"Oh, no? Well, she's awfully good at *looking* old!" Nancy snapped.

"Yes, I know," nodded Old Tom. "It all started when she had trouble with her boyfriend. Ever since, she's been bitter and hard to deal with."

"That's for sure," said Nancy, indignantly. "There's no way to please her, no matter how hard you try! I'd leave if my family didn't need the money. But someday I may just boil over and tell her how I feel. And then of course it'll be 'Goodbye, Nancy' for me."

Old Tom shook his head sadly. "I know how you feel. But believe me, that would be a mistake."

"Nancy!" called a sharp voice.

"Yes, ma'am," Nancy answered, hurrying toward the house.

G · L · A · D

Chapter 3

The Coming of Pollyanna

On June 24th, a telegram came, announcing Pollyanna's arrival the next afternoon at 4 o'clock. Miss Polly read the telegram, frowned, and then climbed the stairs up to the attic room. She still frowned as she looked around the room. There was a small bed, two straight-backed chairs, a dresser without a mirror, and a small table. There were no pictures on the wall. And there were no curtains at the small windows, which were kept closed because they had no screens. The little room was as hot as an oven. A big fly was buzzing angrily at one of the windows, trying to get out. Miss Polly killed the fly, straightened a chair, frowned again, and left the room.

"Nancy," she said, standing at the kitchen door. "I found a fly in Miss Pollyanna's room. I have ordered screens, but until they come I expect you to make sure that the windows stay closed. I want you to meet my niece tomorrow at the train station. Timothy will drive you over in the open carriage. The telegram said she has light-colored hair, and is wearing a red-checked dress and a straw hat. That is all I know about her."

"Yes, ma'am. But . . . but . . . aren't you . . ."

Miss Polly frowned and said crisply, "No, I am not going. I don't think that's necessary. That will be all, Nancy." And she walked away.

Nancy slammed her iron down on the ironing board and thought to herself, *Well, I'd be ashamed to admit that's all I knew about my only niece!*

The next afternoon, Timothy, Old Tom's son, drove Nancy to the station. Although they had become good friends, Nancy was too worried to chat as much as she usually did. Over and over she said to herself, "light-colored hair, red-checked dress, straw hat." And over and over she wondered just what kind of child this Pollyanna would turn out to be.

"I hope for her sake that she's quiet and sensible, and doesn't drop knives or bang doors," Nancy sighed as they reached the station.

Timothy grinned. "Well, if she isn't, who knows what'll become of the rest of us? Can you imagine Miss Polly with a *noisy* kid? Golly! There's the train whistle now!"

Soon Nancy saw her—a slender little girl in a red-checked dress, with two fat braids of golden hair hanging down her back. Under the straw hat, her eager, freckled little face turned from side to side, clearly searching for someone.

With shaking knees, Nancy went over to the child. "Are you Miss Pollyanna?" she asked timidly.

Instantly the child threw her arms around her. "Oh, I'm so glad, glad, *glad* to see you!" she exclaimed eagerly. "Of course I'm Pollyanna, and I'm so glad you came to meet me! I hoped you would."

"You hoped *I'd* come to meet you?" Nancy asked, puzzled.

"Oh, yes. I've been wondering all the way here what you looked like," exclaimed the little girl, dancing on her toes. "And now that I know, I'm glad you look just the way you do."

Still confused by Pollyanna's words, Nancy introduced Timothy and asked if Pollyanna had a trunk.

"Yes, I do," nodded Pollyanna proudly. "I've got a brand-new one. The Ladies' Aid bought it for me. And wasn't that lovely of them, when what they really wanted was a red carpet for the church? Of course, I don't know how much red carpet they could have bought with the money they spent on my trunk. But I'd guess it would have bought some. What do you think—maybe half an aisle? Oh, and I've got a little thing in my bag that Mr. Gray said was a check, and that I must give it to you to claim my trunk. Mr. Gray is Mrs. Gray's husband. They're cousins of Deacon Carr's wife. I came east with them, and they're lovely! And—oh, here it is," Pollyanna said, after fumbling in her bag. She handed the slip to Nancy.

After Timothy loaded the trunk into the carriage, Pollyanna snuggled into the seat between Nancy and Timothy. The entire time, Pollyanna never stopped talking. Nancy was out of breath, just trying to keep up with her chatter.

"Well," Pollyanna said as they drove off. "Isn't this lovely? Is it far? I hope it is. I love to ride. Of course, if it isn't far, I won't mind, because then I'll be glad to get there that much sooner. What a pretty street! I knew it was going to be pretty. Father told me . . ."

At the thought of her father, Pollyanna stopped talking with a little choking breath. Her small chin was trembling, and her eyes were full of tears. After a moment, though, Pollyanna lifted her head bravely and hurried on with her story.

"Father told me all about it. Oh, and I should have explained before. Mrs. Gray told me to, right away. About this red-checked dress, you know. I mean, why I'm not dressed in black. She said you'd think it was wrong. But there weren't any black dresses in the last missionary barrel—only a lady's black velvet jacket. But Deacon Carr's wife said it wasn't appropriate for me at all. And besides, it had white spots on both elbows—you know, from being worn a lot already. Part of the Ladies' Aid wanted to buy me a black dress and hat. But the other part thought that the money should be used to buy the red carpet—for the church, you know. Mrs. White said maybe it was just as well, you know, because she doesn't like children wearing black clothes. I mean, she likes children, of course—just not the black part."

Pollyanna paused for breath—just long enough for Nancy to say, "Well, I'm sure it'll be all right."

"I'm glad you feel that way, too," Pollyanna agreed. "If I had to wear black, it would be a lot harder to be glad . . ."

"Glad!" Nancy gasped, surprised that this orphaned child could feel glad for anything.

"Yes, glad—now that Father's gone to be with Mother and the rest of the children, you know. He said I must be glad. But it's been pretty hard to do—even in a red-checked dress—because— because I wanted so much to have him here with me. Mother and the others already have each other. But without Father, all I have is the Ladies' Aid. But now I'm sure it'll be easier to be glad because now I've got you, Aunt Polly!"

Nancy's sympathy for Pollyanna suddenly turned into terror. "Oh, but you've made a terrible mistake! I'm only Nancy. I'm not your Aunt Polly at all!"

"You—you—aren't?" Pollyanna asked in dismay.

"No. I'm only Nancy, the hired girl. And I'm not a bit like your Aunt Polly. Not at all!"

"But there *is* an Aunt Polly, isn't there?" the child asked anxiously.

"There sure is!" Timothy exclaimed.

Polly, relieved, said nothing for a moment. Then she continued brightly, "And you know I'm glad, after all, that she didn't come to meet me. This way I got to spend time with you—and I can still look forward to seeing *her*, too! You know she's the only aunt I've got. And I didn't even know I had her for a long time. Then Father told me. He said she lived in a great big lovely house 'way on top of a hill."

"It's that big white one up ahead," said Nancy, pointing.

"Oh, how pretty! I've never seen so many trees and green grass all in one place. Nancy, is my Aunt Polly rich?"

"Yes, Miss."

"I'm so glad. It must be perfectly lovely to have lots of money. I've never known anyone who did— except for the Whites. They have carpets in every room and ice cream sundaes. Does Aunt Polly have ice cream sundaes?"

Nancy glanced at Timothy and tried not to giggle. "No, Miss. I don't think your aunt likes ice cream. At least, I've never seen any on her table."

Pollyanna's face fell in disappointment. "Oh, she doesn't? I'm so sorry! How can she not like ice cream? Well, I can be kind of glad for that, because if you don't eat ice cream, it can't make your stomach ache—like Mrs. White's ice cream did—when I ate hers—you know, lots of it. Maybe at least Aunt Polly has carpets?"

"Yes."

"In every room?"

"Well, in almost every room," Nancy answered. She frowned as she thought about that bare little attic room where there was no carpet.

"Oh, I'm so glad!" exclaimed Pollyanna. "I love carpets. We didn't have any—only two little rugs that came in a missionary barrel. And one of those had ink spots on it. Mrs. White had pictures, too. Don't you just love pictures? I do. We didn't have any pictures, though. They don't often come in the missionary barrels. One time, though, two pictures came. But one was so good that Father sold it to get money to buy me shoes. And the other one was so bad that it fell apart just as soon as we hung it up. And I cried. But now I'm glad we didn't have any of those nice things, 'cause now I'll like Aunt Polly's even better. You know, since I'm not used to them. My, isn't this a perfectly beautiful house!" Pollyanna exclaimed as they turned into the wide driveway.

Nancy tried to imagine how Pollyanna and Miss Polly would manage to live together. "Well, if that poor child needs someone to turn to for comfort, then I'm going to be there for her," thought Nancy, as she led Pollyanna in the wide front door.

The Little Attic Room

Miss Polly Harrington did not bother to stand up to greet her niece. Instead, she simply looked up from her book and dutifully held out a hand. "How do you do, Pollyanna?" she said coldly. "I . . ."

Before she could finish, Pollyanna flew across the room. To Miss Polly's shock and dismay, Pollyanna threw herself right into her aunt's lap.

"Oh, Aunt Polly, Aunt Polly, I don't know how to be glad enough that you're letting me come live with you," she sobbed. "You don't know how perfectly lovely it is to have you and Nancy instead of just the Ladies' Aid!"

"Indeed," Miss Polly answered stiffly, trying to unclasp Pollyanna's small, clinging fingers. She frowned at Nancy. "Nancy, that will do. You may go. Pollyanna, please stand up properly so I can see what you look like."

Pollyanna pulled away anxiously. "I'm afraid I'm not much to look at because of my freckles. Oh, and I should explain about the red-checked dress and the black velvet jacket with white spots on the elbows. I told Nancy how Father said . . ."

"Never mind what your father said," interrupted Miss Polly, crisply. "You have a trunk, I suppose?"

"Oh, yes, indeed, Aunt Polly. I've got a beautiful trunk that the Ladies' Aid gave me. I don't have much in it—of my own, I mean. But there were all of Father's books. And Mrs. White said she thought I should have them. You see, Father . . ."

"Pollyanna," interrupted her aunt again, sharply. "There is one thing that must be understood right away. And that is, I do not wish to hear any more about your father."

The little girl gasped. "You mean—you mean . . ."

"I mean now we'll go upstairs to your room. You may follow me, Pollyanna."

Without a word, Pollyanna turned and followed her aunt. Her eyes brimmed with tears, but her chin was bravely high. Pollyanna told herself, *I guess I'm glad she doesn't want me to talk about Father. Maybe she's thinks that talking about him would make me sad.*

Pollyanna looked around at the lacy curtains

and gold picture frames. The plush green carpet was as soft as moss. "Oh, Aunt Polly! Aunt Polly! What a perfectly lovely, lovely house! You must be very glad to be so rich!"

"Why, Pollyanna!" scolded her aunt. "How could you say such a thing? I would never take pride in my riches. That would be a sin!"

Miss Polly was glad that her niece would be in the attic room. At first, her plan was to keep the child as far away as possible. Now she was glad that the attic was so plain and sensible. It would make Pollyanna less vain, and keep her from destroying expensive furniture.

Pollyanna couldn't wait to see her own dear room. She imagined how beautiful it would be—full of soft rugs, pretty curtains, sparkling pictures.

Then her aunt led her up another flight of stairs and threw open a door. "Here is your room, Pollyanna. And there is your trunk. Do you have the key to it?"

It was so hot in the room that Pollyanna could hardly breathe. Her eyes were wide and frightened. She nodded her head.

Her aunt frowned. "When I ask a question, Pollyanna, I want you to answer it out loud, not merely with your head."

"Yes, Aunt Polly."

"Thank you. That is better. I believe you have everything you need. I will send Nancy up to help you unpack. Dinner is at 6 o'clock." Miss Polly turned and briskly left the room.

Pollyanna stared at the bare windows, the bare walls, the bare floor. Her eyes filled with tears as she stumbled toward the little trunk that used to be in her own little room in that faraway Western home. She knelt beside it, covering her face with her hands.

When Nancy came into the room a few minutes later, she tried to comfort the little girl. But Pollyanna only shook her head and sobbed. "But I'm so ashamed of myself, Nancy. I just can't understand why my father had to leave me to join my mother."

Wiping tears from her own eyes, Nancy said, "Well, together we'll get your dresses unpacked in no time."

Embarrassed, Pollyanna admitted, "There aren't many dresses."

"Then we'll have them unpacked even faster," Nancy said cheerfully.

Suddenly, Pollyanna smiled brightly. "That's right! Now I can be glad for that, can't I?"

Nancy stared, not sure what to say. She quickly unpacked the books and the sad-looking dresses covered with patches.

Smiling bravely now, Pollyanna helped put away the books and clothing. After a while, she said, a little uncertainly, "I'm sure it's going to be a very nice room. Don't you think so, Nancy?"

Nancy didn't answer.

"And I can be glad there's no mirror here," Pollyanna continued. "That way, I don't have to see my freckles."

Nancy said nothing, choking back a sob.

Pollyanna ran over to the window and clapped her hands in joy. "Oh, Nancy! I hadn't seen this before. Look—'way over there are such lovely trees and houses and a river shining just like silver. Who needs pictures with a view like that? Oh, now I'm really glad she let me have this room!"

To Pollyanna's surprise and dismay, Nancy burst into tears.

"What is it, Nancy? This wasn't *your* room, was it?"

"*My* room!" stormed Nancy angrily, choking back the tears. "Oh, no! There's her bell!" Nancy said, as she jumped up, dashed out of the room, and ran down the stairs.

Pollyanna went back to what she now thought of as her "picture"—the beautiful view from the window. That afternoon, the room was so hot she could hardly stand it. Timidly, she touched the window frame. To her joy, the window flew wide open. Soon Pollyanna was leaning far out, drinking in the fresh, sweet air.

She ran to the other window and opened it eagerly. A big fly swept past her nose and buzzed noisily around the room. Then another fly came,

and another. But Pollyanna didn't notice, for she had made a wonderful discovery. A large tree stretched its great branches up against the window. They looked like big arms, reaching out to her, inviting her.

Suddenly, Pollyanna laughed out loud. "I think I can do it," she chuckled as she stepped onto the window ledge. From there, she reached the nearest branch and quickly climbed down to the lowest limb. The drop to the ground was a little scary, even for Pollyanna, who was used to climbing trees. She took a deep breath and landed in the soft grass.

Pollyanna looked around eagerly. There, in back of the house, was a garden, where an old man bent over his work. Beyond the garden, a little path led through an open field and up a steep hill. At the top of the hill, a single pine tree stood guarding a large rock. There was only one place in the world where Pollyanna wanted to be at that moment—on top of that big rock.

Pollyanna skipped past the old man and across the open field. With great determination, she began to climb. But the rock that had seemed so near the house now started to look far, far away.

Fifteen minutes later, the grandfather clock in the Harrington house struck six. Exactly as the last chime sounded, Nancy rang the bell for dinner.

One, two, three minutes passed. Miss Polly frowned and tapped the floor with her foot. Then she went into the hall, looked up the stairs impatiently, and listened carefully. Finally she turned and swept back into the dining room

"Nancy," she said severely, "my niece is late. I told her what time dinner was, and now she will have to suffer the consequences. She must learn to be on time. When she comes down, she may have bread and milk in the kitchen."

"Yes, ma'am," Nancy answered, trying not to show her anger.

After dinner, Nancy sneaked upstairs to check on Pollyanna. But Pollyanna was gone! Nancy ran out to tell Old Tom, who was still working in the garden.

Old Tom looked out at the land all around him. Finally he stopped and pointed his finger. There, against the reddening sunset sky, was a tiny, wind-blown girl, perched on top of a large rock.

Turning to Old Tom, Nancy said, "If Miss Polly asks, tell her I haven't forgotten about the dishes, but that I've gone on a walk." Then she turned and hurried along the path that led across the open field.

Chapter 5

The Game

"*Y*ou gave me quite a scare, Miss Pollyanna!" Nancy panted, as she hurried up to the big rock.

"Scare? Oh, I'm so sorry, Nancy. But you don't have to worry about me. I always come back all right."

"But I didn't even know you'd gone away," said Nancy, taking Pollyanna's hand and hurrying down the hill. "How did you slip out of the house without being seen?"

"Oh, I didn't slip at all. I just climbed down the tree and then jumped to the ground."

"Oh, my!" gasped Nancy. "I'd sure like to know what your aunt would say about that!"

"You would? Then I'll just tell her so you can find out," the little girl promised cheerfully.

"Oh, dear, no! Don't do that!" Nancy

exclaimed, hoping to keep Pollyanna from being scolded by her aunt.

"Why? Do you think she'd care if I climbed down trees?"

"Well, no. Rather—yes. I mean—I guess I don't really know what she'd say," Nancy answered. "Anyway, I've got to hurry up and get the dishes done."

"I'll help you," Pollyanna promised.

As the sky grew darker, Pollyanna held her new friend's hand more tightly and shivered. "I guess I'm glad, after all, that you *did* get a little scared—'cause then you came to get me."

"Oh, you poor thing! Now I'm afraid you'll have to eat bread and milk in the kitchen with me. Your aunt was unhappy that you didn't come down to dinner."

"But how could I? I was up here. Anyway, I'm glad."

"Glad! Why?"

"Because I like bread and milk, and I'd like to eat with you. What's wrong with being glad for that?"

"Nothing. But you seem glad for *everything!*"

Pollyanna laughed. "Well, that's the game, you know."

"The *game?*"

"Yes. The 'Just Being Glad' game. Father taught it to me, and it's lovely," answered

Pollyanna. "We played it ever since I was a little girl. Then I taught it to the Ladies' Aid, and some of them played it, too."

"How do you play it?"

Pollyanna laughed again, but then she sighed a little wistfully. "We started playing it when the crutches came in a missionary barrel."

"*Crutches!*"

"Yes. You see, I'd wanted a doll. And my father had asked them to send us one. But instead, the barrel had a letter inside saying they didn't have any dolls. So they sent children's crutches instead, thinking they might come in handy sometime. And that's when we began playing the game."

"So what makes that a game?" Nancy asked, still upset that Pollyanna hadn't received a doll.

"Well, the game was to find something about everything to be glad for—no matter what it was," explained Pollyanna seriously. "So we began playing right then—on the crutches."

"But I can't see anything to be glad about—getting a pair of crutches when you wanted a doll!"

Pollyanna clapped her hands in delight. "But there is! There is! Of course, I couldn't see it at first, either, Nancy. Father had to explain it to me."

"Then I guess you'll have to tell me, too," Nancy said.

"Why, just be glad because *you don't need*

them!" Pollyanna shouted, triumphantly. "You see. It's really easy—once you know how!"

"Well, I never . . ." Nancy said in disbelief.

"Oh, but anybody can play the game. And the harder it is, the more fun it is. Only sometimes it's almost too hard, like when your father dies and there's nobody left except a Ladies' Aid."

"Or when you're put into a bare little room 'way up in the hot attic," Nancy growled.

Pollyanna sighed. "Yes, that was a hard one at first," she admitted. "Especially since I was so lonely and wanted to have pretty things in my room. But then I thought about how I hate to see my freckles in mirrors. And I saw that lovely picture out the window. So then I knew I'd found things to be glad for. And once you start hunting for things to be glad for, you sort of forget about the things you wanted and can't have."

Nancy choked back her tears and said nothing.

"I'm so used to playing the game that now I can often think of things without even trying. It's a lovely game. Father and I used to like it so much." Pollyanna sighed and tried bravely not to cry. "I guess it'll be a little harder now, since I don't have anybody to play it with." Then Pollyanna smiled. "Maybe Aunt Polly will play it!"

Nancy gasped, trying to imagine *Miss Polly* playing the game. Then she said, "I'm not sure

I'll be able to play it very well, but I promise I'll play it with you."

"Oh, Nancy!" Pollyanna shouted, giving her a hug. "That's wonderful! Won't we have fun?"

"Well—maybe," Nancy said, not sure at all. "At least you'll have *someone* to play it with, anyhow."

They went into the kitchen, and Pollyanna happily ate her bread and milk. Then she went into the living room, where her aunt sat reading. Miss Polly looked up coldly.

"Have you had your dinner, Pollyanna?"

"Yes, Aunt Polly."

"I'm very sorry, Pollyanna, that I had to make you eat just bread and milk in the kitchen."

"But I was really glad you did it, Aunt Polly. I like bread and milk. And I like being with Nancy in the kitchen. You don't have to feel bad at all about doing that."

Aunt Polly suddenly sat up taller in her chair. "Pollyanna," she said firmly, "it's time for you to go to bed. Tomorrow we will plan your daily activities. Breakfast will be at 7:30. Make sure you are down in time. Now, goodnight."

Pollyanna ran over to her aunt and gave her a loving hug. "I've had such a beautiful time so far," she sighed happily. "I know I'm going to just love living with you. Goodnight!" she called cheerfully, as she ran out of the room.

"My goodness!" exclaimed Miss Polly. "What a most extraordinary child!" Then she frowned. "She said that she's 'glad' I punished her. And she's going to 'love living' with me! Incredible!" And then Miss Polly went back to her book and forgot all about Pollyanna.

Meanwhile, all alone in her attic room, Pollyanna sobbed into her sheets. "I know, Father, that I'm not playing the game right now. But I don't think even *you* could find anything to be glad for being 'way up here, all alone in the dark. If only I could be near Nancy or Aunt Polly—or even a Ladies' Aider!"

Downstairs in the kitchen, Nancy washed out the milk pitcher and muttered, "If the only way to help that poor child is to play a silly game about being glad you've got crutches when you really wanted dolls—well, then, I'll play it, I will!"

Chapter 6

A Question of Duty

It was almost 7:00 when Pollyanna woke up the next morning. Hearing the birds chirping joyfully, Pollyanna rushed to the window to talk to them. She saw that her aunt was already out in the garden, talking to the old man about a rosebush. Excited to greet her aunt, Pollyanna hurried down the attic steps, leaving the doors wide open.

Pollyanna threw her arms around her aunt, bubbling with delight. "Oh, Aunt Polly! I'm so glad this morning just to be alive!"

"*Pollyanna!*" the lady scolded sternly. She tried to straighten herself with dignity, even though Pollyanna was still hanging onto her neck. "Is this the usual way you say 'good morning'?"

"Oh, no," answered Pollyanna. She let go of her aunt and began dancing lightly up and down.

"Only when I love people so much that I just can't help it! I saw you from my window, Aunt Polly. And I got to thinking how you weren't a Ladies' Aider, and you were really, truly my aunt. And you looked so good I just had to come down and hug you!"

Miss Polly found she couldn't frown as easily as usual. So she turned and walked away.

Turning to the bent old man, Pollyanna asked, "Do you always work in the garden, Mr.—uh—?"

"Yes, Miss. I'm Old Tom, the gardener," he answered, trying not to laugh, but also blinking back tears. "You are so like your mother, little Miss! I knew her when she was even littler than you."

"You did? You knew my mother when she was alive? Oh, please tell me about her!"

Just then, a bell rang outside the house. The next moment, Nancy flew out the back door.

"Miss Pollyanna, that bell means it's mealtime." Nancy grabbed Pollyanna's hand and hurried her back to the house. "Whenever you hear it—no matter where you are—you must run home as fast as you can. Because if you don't— well, then it would take someone a lot smarter than us to find *anything* to be glad about then!" With that, Nancy shooed Pollyanna into the house the way she would shoo a straying chicken into a coop.

At first, breakfast was a silent meal. Then Miss Polly, watching with disapproval as two flies lightly darted here and there over the table, said sternly, "Nancy, where did those flies come from?"

"I don't know, ma'am. There weren't any flies in the kitchen."

"I guess maybe they're my flies, Aunt Polly," Pollyanna said pleasantly. "There were lots of them upstairs this morning, having a beautiful time."

"*Yours!*" gasped Miss Polly. "What do you mean? Where did they come from?"

"Why, Aunt Polly," explained Pollyanna, surprised that her aunt didn't know. "They came from outside, of course—through the open windows."

"You mean you opened windows without screens?"

"Why, yes, Aunt Polly. There aren't any screens in my windows."

"Nancy," Miss Polly ordered sharply. "Go right now to Miss Pollyanna's room and shut the windows. Shut the doors, also. Then after your morning work is done, go through every room with the fly swatter. Be sure you search very thoroughly."

Then Miss Polly turned to her niece. "Pollyanna, I knew, of course, that it was my duty to order screens for those windows. But until they arrive, you must remember *your* duty, as well."

"My—*duty*?" Pollyanna asked, not understanding.

"Indeed. I know it is warm. But it is still your duty to keep your windows closed until those screens come. Flies are not only dirty and annoying. They are very dangerous to one's health. After breakfast, I will give you a little pamphlet to read about this matter."

"Oh, thank you, Aunt Polly. I love to read!"

Miss Polly gasped. Then she shut her lips together tightly. Pollyanna noticed her aunt's stern expression and apologized timidly. "Of course, I'm sorry that I forgot about my duty. I won't open the windows again."

Miss Polly did not speak again until the meal was over. Then she got up, went to the bookcase in the living room, took out a small pamphlet, and placed it on the table next to her niece. "This is the article I mentioned, Pollyanna. I want you to go to your room right away and read it. I will be up in half an hour to check on you."

Pollyanna looked at the cover. She was delighted to see a fly's head, magnified many times. "Oh, thank you, Aunt Polly!" she exclaimed with delight. Then she skipped merrily out of the room, banging the door behind her.

Miss Polly frowned and was about to scold Pollyanna, but her niece was already racing up the attic stairs.

Half an hour later, Miss Polly dutifully climbed up those same stairs and entered Pollyanna's room. Her stern face was greeted with a burst of eager enthusiasm.

"Oh, Aunt Polly! I've never seen anything so perfectly lovely and interesting in my whole life! I'm so glad you gave me that booklet to read! I had no idea that flies could carry so many dirty things on their feet, and . . ."

"That will do," interrupted Aunt Polly, with dignity. "Pollyanna, you may show me the clothes you've brought with you. Then I'll decide if they're suitable."

Pollyanna sighed. "I'm afraid you'll think they're even worse than the Ladies' Aiders did. And they said they were shameful. You see, in the last few barrels, there were mostly things for boys and old people. Did you ever get a missionary barrel, Aunt Polly?"

Pollyanna noticed her aunt's look of shocked anger. Blushing, she rushed to correct her mistake. "Why, no. Of course, you didn't Aunt Polly. I forgot that rich people don't have to get them. But you see, sometimes when I'm 'way up here in this room, I kind of forget that you are rich."

Miss Polly looked indignant, but was unable to speak. Pollyanna, unaware that she had said anything offensive, hurried on. "Anyway, the thing about missionary barrels is that they never have what you think they will. That's why it was hardest to play the game with missionary barrels, at least for Father and . . ."

Just in time, Pollyanna remembered that she wasn't supposed to talk about her father. So she turned and gathered up the ragged little dresses she had brought with her. "They aren't nice at all," she choked. "But they're all I've got."

In disgust, Miss Polly picked up each dress by her fingertips and looked it over. Then she turned abruptly to her niece. "You have been to school, haven't you, Pollyanna?"

"Oh, yes, Aunt Polly. But mostly Fath—I mean, I was mostly taught at home."

Miss Polly frowned. "Very well. In the fall, you will enter school here, of course. Meanwhile, I suppose I ought to hear you read aloud one half hour every day."

"I love to read. But if you don't want to listen to me, I'd be just as glad to read to myself. It would be easier to be glad for that, since I'm not always sure of the big words."

"Indeed," said Miss Polly, grimly. "Have you studied music?"

"Not much. I like other people's music better than my own."

"Very likely," said Aunt Polly, raising her eyebrows. "Nevertheless, I think it is my duty to see that you have proper lessons. You sew, of course?"

"Yes, ma'am," Pollyanna sighed. "But it was really hard for me to learn. You see, each Ladies' Aider taught me a different way of sewing and ..."

"Well, that will no longer be a problem, Pollyanna. I shall teach you sewing myself, of course. You do not know how to cook, I assume."

"They were just starting to teach me this summer. I'd just learned only how to make chocolate fudge when Fa—when I had to stop." Pollyanna choked back the tears.

"Chocolate fudge, indeed!" said Miss Polly scornfully. "Well then. At 9 o'clock every morning you will read aloud to me for one half hour. At 9:30 on Wednesday and Saturday mornings, you will spend time with Nancy in the kitchen, learning how to cook. Other mornings you will sew with me. Then you will spend the rest of the afternoons with a music teacher."

Pollyanna cried out in dismay. "Oh, but Aunt Polly! You haven't left me any time at all just to—to live!"

"To live, child! What do you mean? You'd be living while doing those things!"

"Oh, sure. I'd be *breathing*, Aunt Polly. But I wouldn't be *living*. You can breathe while you're asleep. But you're not living then. I mean *living*—doing the things you want, like playing outdoors, reading (to myself, that is), climbing hills, talking to Mr. Tom and Nancy, and finding out all about the houses and the people and everything in those perfectly lovely streets I came through yesterday. That's what I call living, Aunt Polly. Just breathing isn't living!"

Miss Polly raised her eyebrows in irritation. "How ungrateful you are, Pollyanna! I am willing to do my duty by giving you proper care and instruction. So *you* should be willing to do yours by not wasting that care and instruction."

Pollyanna looked shocked. "Oh, Aunt Polly. I could never be ungrateful—especially not to *you!* Why, I *love you!*"

"Very well. Then see that you don't act ungrateful," commanded Miss Polly, as she turned toward the door.

Then Pollyanna asked, in a small, unsteady voice, "Please, Aunt Polly. Tell me which of my dresses I may keep."

Aunt Polly let out a tired sigh. "None of your dresses is fit to wear. We'll have to get rid of them all. I would not be doing my duty if I let you wear them in public."

Now it was Pollyanna who sighed. She was beginning to hate that word "duty." It seemed to make her aunt so tired! "Aunt Polly," she asked hopefully, "isn't there any way you could feel *glad* for being able to do your duty?"

Miss Polly's face darkened. "Don't be rude, Pollyanna!" And she swept angrily down the stairs.

Alone in the hot little attic room, Pollyanna sat down on one of the straight-backed chairs. "What's wrong with trying to find something to be glad for in doing your duty?" she wondered. She looked sadly at the dresses that would be taken away from her. "Maybe there's nothing to be glad for in doing your duty." And then with a sudden laugh she thought, "Except maybe to be glad when your duty's done!"

Chapter
7

Pollyanna and Punishments

$\mathcal{S}$hopping for new clothes was a rewarding experience for everyone involved. Afterwards, Miss Polly felt relieved—as though she were once again on solid ground after walking along the edge of a volcano. The salespeople had enough funny stories about Pollyanna to keep their friends laughing for days. And Pollyanna herself ended up with a glowing smile and a happy heart. As she told one of the salespeople, "After wearing used clothes all your life, it's perfectly lovely just to walk right in and buy clothes that really fit *you!*"

That afternoon, Old Tom told Pollyanna wonderful things about her mother. And that made her really happy. Then Nancy told her all about the little farm where her own dear mother and sisters lived. "And *they've* got lovely names, too," sighed Nancy. "Not like my name. I just hate 'Nancy'!"

"Oh, Nancy! What a horrible thing to say! Why do you hate it?"

"Because it isn't pretty, like 'Florabelle' and 'Estelle.' You see, when I was born, my mother hadn't begun reading stories with pretty names in them."

"But I love 'Nancy,'" declared Pollyanna, "just because it's you!"

"Well," Nancy said gloomily, "you'd love 'Clarissa' just as much—and I'd be a lot happier with that name!"

Pollyanna laughed. "At least you can be glad your name isn't 'Haphzibah.'"

"Haphzibah!"

"Yes. That's Mrs. White's name. Her husband calls her 'Ha' for short. But she doesn't like it. Whenever he calls out 'Ha! Ha!' she thinks he's laughing at her."

Nancy smiled. "I'll never again hear 'Nancy' without thinking 'Ha-Ha' and giggling. I guess I really *am* glad." She looked at Pollyanna in amazement. "So were you playing that game just now?"

Pollyanna thought it over and then laughed. "Why, Nancy, I guess I was! But that time I did it without thinking. You see, once you get used to looking for things to be glad for, you don't even have to think about doing it. And there's almost always something about everything to be glad for. You just have to keep hunting long enough to find it.

"Well, maybe," said Nancy, not really believing Pollyanna.

At 8:30, Pollyanna went to bed. The screens hadn't come yet, and the little room was like an oven. Pollyanna looked longingly at the two tightly closed windows. But she didn't dare raise them. She climbed into bed, but tossed from side to side in sleepless misery. All around here was velvet blackness, except for a silvery path cast by the moon. Finally Pollyanna got up and followed that path to one of the windows. Outside the world looked magical and beautiful. She thought about how good the fresh, sweet air would feel on her hot cheeks and hands.

Then she saw the flat roof over the sunroom. It was just below her window. If only she could sleep there, in the moonlight and the cool, sweet night air! And sometimes people *had* to sleep outside—like Joel Hartley, when he was sick.

Pollyanna happily raised the window, grabbed her sheets, and tossed them onto the roof below. Then she slid out the window. But before dropping to the roof below, she carefully closed the window behind her. Pollyanna had not forgotten about those flies with the wonderful little feet that carried things!

How deliciously cool it was! Pollyanna danced up and down in delight, enjoying the crackling sounds that the roof made under her feet. Then she spread out her sheets and lay down to sleep.

"I'm so glad that the screens didn't come yet," she thought, blinking up at the stars. "For then I wouldn't have done this!"

Downstairs, in her room next to the sunroom, Miss Polly hurried into her bathrobe and slippers. Her face was pale and frightened. With a shaking voice, she telephoned Timothy. "Come quickly— and bring your father. There's someone on the roof of the sunroom. He must have climbed up from the garden. And from the sunroom roof he'll be able to get right into the house!"

A few minutes later, Pollyanna was awakened by a flashlight in her eyes. Startled, she exclaimed, "Mr. Tom! Aunt Polly! Don't look so scared. I'm not sick or anything, like Joel Hartley. It's just that I was so hot inside. But don't worry, Aunt Polly. I remembered to shut the windows so the flies wouldn't carry in germs on their feet."

"Pollyanna," Miss Polly said sternly. "Hand me your sheets and come inside at once. Of all the . . ." Miss Polly muttered under her breath.

Pollyanna sighed sadly, but she did not complain.

Once inside, Miss Polly said stiffly, "For the rest of the night, Pollyanna, you will sleep in my bed with me. The screens will be here tomorrow. But until then it is my duty to keep you where I know you'll be safe."

Pollyanna gasped. "With you? In your bed?" she asked joyously. "Oh, Aunt Polly! Aunt Polly!

How perfectly lovely of you! I've always wanted to sleep with someone who belongs to me! I sure am glad now that those screens didn't come! Wouldn't you be, too?"

Miss Polly marched on ahead, not knowing what to say. This was the third time she tried to punish Pollyanna. But once again Pollyanna looked at her punishment as some kind of reward. No wonder Miss Polly was feeling strangely powerless.

Pollyanna Pays a Visit

$\mathcal{S}$oon life at the Harrington home settled into a sort of routine—though not exactly the routine that Miss Polly had at first expected. Pollyanna did, in fact, sew, practice her music, read aloud, and study cooking. But she ended up spending less time on these activities than originally planned. And that gave her more time to "just live." Most afternoons she was free from 2 until 6 to do what she wanted—as long as she didn't want to do things that Aunt Polly had already forbidden.

Why did Aunt Polly end up allowing Pollyanna so much free time? Was it to give Pollyanna a break from working? Or to give her aunt a break from Pollyanna? It is true that each reading and sewing lesson left Miss Polly completely dazed and exhausted. Nancy, though, always looked forward to her time with Pollyanna in the kitchen.

Pollyanna didn't mind that there were no children nearby. As she explained to Nancy, "I'm happy just to walk around and watch the people. I just love people. Don't you, too, Nancy?

"Well—not all of them," replied Nancy.

When the weather was nice, Pollyanna begged to run errands so she could walk outside. On one of these walks, Pollyanna met "the Man." This Man looked different from other men. He wore a long black coat and a fancy hat. He walked stiffly and rather quickly. And he was always alone, which made Pollyanna feel sorry for him. So one day she decided to speak to him.

"How do you do, sir?" she asked cheerily. "Isn't this a nice day?"

The man looked around in surprise. Seeing only Pollyanna, he asked in a sharp voice, "Were you speaking to *me*?"

"Yes, sir," Pollyanna smiled. "I said, it's a nice day, isn't it?"

"Eh? Oh! Humph!" he grunted and walked away.

Pollyanna laughed. He was such a funny man!

The next day when she saw him again, she called out cheerfully, "It's not quite as nice a day as yesterday. But it's still pretty nice."

"Eh? Oh! Humph!" he grunted as before. And again Pollyanna laughed happily.

The next time Pollyanna greeted him the

same way, the man stopped abruptly. "Look here, child. Who are you? And why are you speaking to me every day?"

"I'm Pollyanna Whittier. And I thought you looked lonely. I'm so glad you stopped. Now we've been introduced. But I don't know your name yet."

"Well, of all the . . ." the man muttered, and walked away faster than ever.

Pollyanna's smile drooped with disappointment. "Maybe he didn't realize that we never finished our introduction," she thought, and then continued on her errand.

Pollyanna was taking some ham to Mrs. Snow today. Once a week, Miss Polly sent Mrs. Snow something to eat. She said it was her duty, since Mrs. Snow was poor, sick, and a member of her church. So every Thursday, Miss Polly did her duty—not personally, but through Nancy. Today Pollyanna begged for the privilege of taking the gift to Mrs. Snow.

Nancy admitted to Pollyanna, "I'm glad I don't have to do it myself. But it's a shame to dump that job on you, poor child."

"But I'd love to do it, Nancy."

"Well, you won't. Not after you've done it once," Nancy said sourly.

"Why not?

"Because nobody does. The only reason people visit Mrs. Snow is that they feel sorry for her. That's how nasty she is. I sure pity her daughter, who *has* to take care of her."

"But what's she like, Nancy?"

"Well, she's never satisfied with what's going on. If it's Monday, then she wishes it were Sunday. And if you take her ham, she'll tell you she wanted chicken. But if you *did* bring her chicken, she'd just be longing for lamb!"

"What a funny woman," laughed Pollyanna. "I think I'd like to go see her. She must be so surprising and—well, different. I love people who are different."

"Well, Mrs. Snow's 'different,' all right. At least, I hope there aren't other people like her," Nancy grumbled.

As Pollyanna opened the gate of Mrs. Snow's run-down little house, her eyes sparkled at the thought of meeting someone "different."

A pale and tired-looking young woman answered the door.

"How do you do?" Pollyanna began politely. "Miss Polly Harrington sent me. I'd like to see Mrs. Snow, please."

Then you're the first person who's ever 'liked' seeing her, the young woman thought as she led Pollyanna down the hall and opened a door.

The room was so dark that Pollyanna blinked for a moment before her eyes adjusted to the gloom. Then she saw a woman propped up in a bed. Pollyanna walked right up to her.

"How do you do, Mrs. Snow? Aunt Polly says she hopes you're feeling comfortable today. And she's sent you a nice piece of ham."

"Oh, dear. Ham, you say? Of course, I am very grateful. But I was hoping it might be lamb today."

Pollyanna looked puzzled. "Why, I thought it was *chicken* you wanted when people brought you ham."

"What?" the sick woman asked sharply.

"Oh, it's nothing," Pollyanna said quickly, trying to please Mrs. Snow. "And of course, it really doesn't make any difference. It's just that Nancy said when we brought ham, you always wanted chicken. But maybe it was the other way, and Nancy had forgotten."

For the first time in weeks, the sick woman

sat up straight in bed. "Well, Miss Boldness. Who are you?" she demanded.

"Oh, my name's not 'Miss Boldness.' And I'm so glad it isn't. Why, that would be worse than 'Haphzibah,' wouldn't it? No. I'm Pollyanna Whittier, Miss Polly Harrington's niece. And I've come to live with her. That's why I'm here this morning with this nice piece of ham."

Hearing Pollyanna mention ham again, the sick woman collapsed back onto her pillow. "Very well. Thank you. Your aunt is very kind, of course. But my appetite isn't very good this morning. And I was so wanting a piece of lamb. You know, I didn't sleep a wink last night. Not a wink!"

"Well, I wish I never had to sleep," Pollyanna sighed. She put the ham on the little nightstand and sat down in a chair next to the bed. "You lose so much time just sleeping! Don't you agree?"

"Lose time *sleeping?*" the sick woman asked.

"Why, yes. I mean, you could be just living instead. It's such a shame that we can't live at night, too."

Once again, the woman pulled herself upright in bed. "Well, you sure are an amazing child!" she exclaimed. "Go over to that window and open the curtain. I'd like to see what you look like!"

As she got up to open the curtain, Pollyanna sighed sadly, "Oh, dear! Then you'll see my freckles, won't you? And just when I was feeling glad that it was dark, because then you couldn't see them. There! Now you can . . ." Pollyanna opened the curtain and turned around. "Oh my! Now I'm so glad you wanted to see me, because now I can see you, too! They didn't tell me you were so pretty!"

"Me? Pretty?" the woman said bitterly.

"Why, yes. Didn't you know it?" asked Pollyanna in surprise.

"Well, no. I didn't," Mrs. Snow answered sharply. After all, she'd spent the last 15 years of her life wishing things were different. That didn't leave much time to enjoy things as they were.

"Oh, but your eyes are so big and dark. And I love your curly black hair. Why, Mrs. Snow, you really *are* pretty! You'd think so, too, if you looked at yourself in a mirror."

"Mirror!" the sick woman exclaimed, falling back on her pillow. "Why would I look in a mirror when I have to spend all my time flat on my back?"

"Well, then, just let me show you," Pollyanna offered. She skipped over to the dresser and picked up a small mirror. But then she stopped and carefully looked at the sick woman. "Would you mind, please, if I fixed your hair just a little before I let you look in the mirror?"

"Why, I—well, I suppose you may, if you really want to," Mrs. Snow finally agreed. "But it won't stay, you know."

"Oh, thank you. I love to fix people's hair!"

Pollyanna shouted with joy. "I won't do much today, because I can't wait to show you how pretty you are. But some day I'll comb it all out and have a perfectly lovely time with it."

For five minutes, Pollyanna worked swiftly. Expertly she combed loose hair into place and fluffed up curls. Meanwhile, the sick woman frowned and looked unhappy. But in spite of herself, she was feeling a little bit of excitement for the first time in many years.

Pollyanna quickly plucked a pink rose from a nearby vase. Then she tucked it into the dark hair right where it would look best. "There! Now you can look!" And she held out the mirror in triumph.

"Humph!" the sick woman grunted, studying her reflection severely. "I like red roses better than pink ones. But roses soon fade anyway, so what's the difference!"

"But then you should be glad that they fade," laughed Pollyanna. "Because then you can enjoy getting some new ones. I just love your hair fluffed out like that," she finished, looking satisfied. "Don't you?"

"Well—maybe. Still, it won't last, since I have to stay in bed, tossing and turning on the pillow."

"No, it won't last," Pollyanna nodded cheerfully. "But that makes me glad, too—because then I can fix it up again. Anyway, you must be glad that your hair's black. Black shows up so nicely on a pillow!"

"Maybe. But it also shows the gray much earlier," Mrs. Snow snapped back. But even while she was complaining, she kept looking at her face in the mirror.

"Oh, but I love black hair! I'd be so glad if only I had it," Pollyanna sighed.

"Oh, no, you wouldn't! Not if you were me! You wouldn't be glad for having black hair or anything else—not if you had to lie here all day as I do!"

Pollyanna frowned as she thought this over. "Why, I guess it would be kind of hard, then, to be glad for things."

"What's there to be glad for when you're sick in bed all the time? Just try to find even one thing to be glad for!"

To Mrs. Snow's amazement, Pollyanna hopped up and clapped her hands. "Great! That'll be a hard one, won't it? I've got to go now. But I'll think about it all the way home. And maybe the next time I come I'll be able to tell you something. Goodbye. I've had a lovely time. Goodbye!" she called again, as she skipped out the door.

"Well, I never! What in the world did she mean by all that?" Mrs. Snow muttered, staring after her visitor. Then she picked up the mirror again, and looked critically at her reflection. "One thing's for sure, though. That little girl has a real talent for doing hair. Why, I never knew it could look so pretty. But then, what's the use?" she sighed, dropping the mirror on the covers and rolling her head on the pillow restlessly.

A little later, Milly, Mrs. Snow's daughter, came into the room to check on her mother. "Why, Mother! The curtain is open!" she exclaimed, staring in amazement at the pink rose in her mother's hair.

"So what if it is?" snapped Mrs. Snow. "Just because I'm sick doesn't mean I have to stay in the dark all my life, does it?"

"Why, no. Of course not," Milly answered quietly, reaching for the medicine bottle. "It's just that I've been trying for ages to open the curtain, but you wouldn't let me."

Mrs. Snow did not answer for a moment. But then she complained, "At least somebody could give me a new nightgown for a change—instead of the same old piece of ham."

"Why, Mother!" Milly gasped, bewildered. In the dresser behind her were two new nightgowns that she'd been trying for months to convince her mother to wear.

Chapter
9

Which Tells of the Man

The next time Pollyanna saw the Man it was raining. But she still greeted him with a bright smile. "It's not so nice out today, is it?" she called lightly. "I'm glad, anyway, that it doesn't rain all the time!"

This time the man didn't turn his head. He didn't even grunt. So Pollyanna assumed, of course, that he hadn't heard her.

So the next day when she saw him, she spoke up more loudly. Pollyanna thought it strange that he was hurrying along, his hands behind his back and his eyes on the ground. Pollyanna didn't understand why he wasn't enjoying the glorious sunshine and the freshly washed morning air.

"How do you do?" she chirped. "I'm so glad it isn't yesterday, aren't you?"

The man stopped abruptly. There was an angry frown on his face. "Now see here, little girl. We might as well settle this thing once and for all. I've got more important things to think about than the weather. I don't pay any attention to whether or not the sun is shining."

Pollyanna's smile widened in joy. "I thought you didn't. That's why I told you, sir!"

"What?"

"I said, I told you about the lovely weather so you'd notice it. I knew you'd be glad the sun was shining if only you stopped to think about it."

"Well, of all the . . ." muttered the man, looking helpless. He started to walk away, but then turned back to Pollyanna, still frowning. "See here. Why don't you find someone your own age to talk to?"

"I'd like to, sir. But there aren't any around here, Nancy says. Still, I don't mind so very much. I like old folks just as much—maybe even more. You see, I'm used to Ladies' Aiders."

"Humph! Ladies' Aiders, indeed! So that's what you think I am? A Ladies' Aider?" The man's lips almost broke into a smile. But his eyes remained grim and stern.

Pollyanna laughed with delight. "Oh, no, sir. You don't look a bit like a Ladies' Aider. Not that you're not as nice, of course—or maybe even nicer." Not wanting to seem impolite, Pollyanna rushed to add, "I mean, I'm sure you're much nicer than you look!"

The man gasped. "Well, of all the . . ." he exclaimed, as he turned and walked briskly away.

The next time Pollyanna met the Man, he looked directly at her, with a pleasant expression on his face. "Good afternoon," he greeted her stiffly. "Perhaps I'd better say right away that I *know* the sun is shining today."

"Oh, but you didn't have to tell me that," Pollyanna nodded brightly. "As soon as I saw you, I *knew* you knew about the sunshine."

"Oh, you did, did you?"

"Yes, sir. I saw it in your eyes. And I saw it in your smile."

"Humph!" grunted the man as he passed on by.

After this, the Man always stopped to speak with Pollyanna. And often he even greeted her first, though usually with just a simple "good afternoon."

But even that was a great surprise to Nancy. "My goodness, Miss Pollyanna!" she gasped one day, when she saw the Man greet Pollyanna. "Did that man actually *speak* to *you?*"

"Why, yes. He always does—now," Pollyanna smiled.

"He *does?* Goodness! Do you know who he is?" Nancy demanded.

Pollyanna frowned and shook her head. "I guess he just forgot. You see, I did my part of the introductions, but he never got around to doing his."

Nancy's eyes widened in amazement. "Why, he's Mr. John Pendleton. He lives all by himself up in that big house on Pendleton Hill. And he never speaks to anybody—except maybe just for business. He has all his meals in the hotel restaurant. My friend Sally Miner waits on him. She says sometimes he doesn't even tell her what he wants to eat. But she knows he'll want something *cheap!*"

Pollyanna nodded in sympathy. "I understand. You have to look for cheap things when you're poor. Father and I used to say how glad we were that we liked beans—especially when we saw how expensive lamb was. Does Mr. Pendleton like beans?"

"Beans? Why, Miss Pollyanna, John Pendleton has loads of money, which he inherited from his father. He's the richest man in town. If he wanted to, he could eat dollar bills. And he wouldn't even notice the difference!"

Pollyanna giggled. "Oh, Nancy. Anybody would notice the difference between beans and dollar bills once they started trying to chew them!"

"I mean he's so rich that having a few dollars more or less wouldn't matter to him. But instead of spending his money, he saves it all."

"Oh, how perfectly lovely!" exclaimed Pollyanna. "Instead of spending it on himself, he saves it to give to the poor!"

Pollyanna's trusting expression made Nancy even angrier about John Pendleton. But instead of taking away Pollyanna's trust, Nancy simply said, "It does seem strange, though, that he talks to you, but he doesn't talk to anyone else. He lives all alone in that great big lovely house, all full of wonderful things. Some people say he's crazy. And some say he's just angry. And some even say he's got a skeleton in his closet."

"Oh, Nancy!" Pollyanna shuddered. "How can he keep such a horrible thing in his closet? Why doesn't he just throw it away?"

Nancy chuckled. "Having a skeleton in his closet means there's a dark secret from his past. He travels a lot, and he writes books. But he never seems to want to spend money here—at least, not for just living."

"Of course not," Pollyanna insisted. "Not if he's saving it for the poor. He sure is a funny man. And he's different, too—like Mrs. Snow. Only he's a different different."

"I guess so," chuckled Nancy.

Pollyanna sighed with satisfaction. "Now I'm gladder than ever that he speaks to me."

Chapter 10

A Surprise for Mrs. Snow

The next time Pollyanna went to see Mrs. Snow, Milly wearily led her down the hall. Once again, the sick woman was lying in a darkened room.

"Oh, dear," the woman complained. "I wish you'd come yesterday. That's when I *wanted* you to come."

"You did? Well, then," Pollyanna laughed cheerfully, "I'm glad it hasn't been more than one day since yesterday! But don't you think it's dark in here? I can't see you at all. Did you fix up your hair the way I did?" Pollyanna asked, as she opened the curtains. "No? Well, never mind. I'm glad you didn't, after all, because maybe you'll let me do it later. But first I want you to see what I brought you."

"Not that it matters how it tastes," she said gloomily. "After all, everything tastes the same when you're ill." Still, she sat up a little so that she could see inside Pollyanna's basket. "Well, what is it?"

"What do you want?" Pollyanna asked, smiling.

The sick woman frowned. "Why, I don't *want* anything."

Pollyanna chuckled. "But if you *did* want something, what would it be?"

The woman didn't know what to say. She was used to wanting what she didn't have. And once she knew what she had, she always knew she wanted something else. But what did she *really* want?

Finally, she suggested, "Well, of course, there's lamb . . ."

"I've got it!" Pollyanna shouted in joy.

"But that's what I *didn't* want," the sick woman sighed, now more sure what her stomach craved. "It was chicken that I wanted."

"Oh, I've got that, too," Pollyanna chuckled.

The woman looked amazed. "Both of them?"

"Yes. And a piece of ham, too!" Pollyanna said triumphantly. "I decided that for once you should have what you wanted. So Nancy and I fixed a little of each. I'm so glad you did want chicken, though. What if you had wanted something else I didn't have—like steak or fish? Wouldn't that have been a shame when I tried so hard?" she laughed merrily.

The woman didn't answer. She was trying to focus on a feeling that was no longer there.

"And how are you today?" Pollyanna asked politely.

"Very poor, thank you," murmured Mrs. Snow, suddenly looking as tired as usual. "I was unable to take a nap this morning. Nellie Higgins next door started taking music lessons. Her practicing drives me crazy. She was at it all morning!"

Pollyanna nodded in sympathy. "I know what you mean. It's *awful!* Mrs. White—one of my Ladies' Aiders—had the same thing. Only she couldn't even roll over to move away from it. Can you?"

Mrs. Snow stared. Then she said in irritation, "Of course, I can move. Anywhere. In bed, that is."

"Well, you can at least be glad of that, can't you? Mrs. White couldn't. She told me she would have gone crazy if it hadn't been for Mr. White's sister's ears."

"Sister's *ears!* What do you mean?"

Pollyanna laughed. "You see, Mr. White's sister is deaf. When she came to help take care of Mrs. White, she couldn't hear the piano next door. So that made Mrs. White feel glad that she *could* hear the piano. She thought it would be much worse to be deaf like Mr. White's sister and not be able to hear anything at all. After that, she didn't mind so much that she *did* hear the piano all the time. You see, she was playing the game, too. I taught her how."

"The game?"

Pollyanna clapped her hands in delight. "I almost forgot. But I thought of something, Mrs. Snow—something you can be glad for."

"*Glad* for! What do you mean?"

"Don't you remember? You asked me to tell you something to be glad for—even though you have to lie here in bed all day."

"Oh, *that!*" snorted the woman. "I didn't think you'd take it seriously."

"Oh, but I *did!*" Pollyanna nodded. "And I found something, too. It was hard. But that made it even more fun. I'll admit that at first I couldn't think of anything. But then I got it."

"Of course, you did," Mrs. Snow said sarcastically. "Well, what is it?"

Pollyanna took a deep breath. Then she stated triumphantly, "I thought you could be glad that other people don't have to be like you—all sick in bed."

"Well, really!" Mrs. Snow exclaimed angrily.

"And now I'll tell you the game," Pollyanna continued, eagerly. "You'll love playing it— especially because it will be so hard for you. And it's so much more fun when it's hard. You see, it's like this."

Pollyanna had just finished telling Mrs. Snow about the crutches and the doll that didn't come, when Milly walked into the room. "Your aunt wants you to hurry home," she said, looking tired and dreary. "She said you've got to finish practicing your music before dark."

Pollyanna sighed. "All right. I'll hurry." Suddenly she laughed. "I guess I should be glad I've got legs to hurry with. Don't you agree, Mrs. Snow?"

The sick woman didn't answer. But there were tears on her cheeks.

"Goodbye!" Pollyanna called, as she left the room. "I'm awfully sorry about not fixing up your hair. I really wanted to do it. But maybe I can the next time."

For the rest of July, the days passed one by one. Pollyanna often told her aunt, joyously, that these were happy days for her. Each time her aunt answered, wearily, "I am pleased that they are happy, Pollyanna. But they must also be profitable. If not, I will have failed in my duty."

Usually Pollyanna answered by giving her aunt a hug and a kiss—which still made Miss Polly feel uncomfortable. But one day Pollyanna asked wistfully, "You mean, then, that it wouldn't be enough if the days were just *happy*?"

"That is what I mean, Pollyanna."

"So they have to be *profitable*, as well?"

"Certainly."

"What makes something *profitable*?"

"Why, it's just profitable. It has profit, something to show for it."

"Then just being glad isn't *profitable*?" Pollyanna asked, worried.

"Certainly not."

"Oh, dear! Then you wouldn't like the game, Aunt Polly. Now I'm afraid you won't ever play the game."

"Game? What game?"

"The game that Father . . ." Pollyanna clapped her hand over her mouth. "Nothing," she said quietly.

Miss Polly frowned. "That will be enough sewing for this morning, Pollyanna," she said sharply. And the lesson was over.

That afternoon, as she was leaving her room, Pollyanna saw her aunt coming up the attic stairs. "Why, Aunt Polly! How perfectly lovely!" she called out. "You were coming up to see me! Come right in. I love company."

But Miss Polly had not been planning to visit her niece. She'd only wanted to get a white sweater that was stored in a box in the attic. But to her surprise, suddenly she was sitting in one of the straight-backed chairs in Pollyanna's little room. Once again, Miss Polly found herself doing something utterly unexpected, something completely different from what she had intended to do. How often something like this occurred—

ever since Pollyanna's arrival!

"I love company," said Pollyanna, trying to be a gracious hostess. "And of course I just *love* this room—even if it doesn't have the pretty rugs and the lace curtains and the lovely pictures . . ." Pollyanna stopped short and blushed.

"What's that, Pollyanna?" her aunt said sharply.

"Nothing, Aunt Polly. Really. I didn't mean to say . . ."

"You probably didn't," said Miss Polly, coldly. "But now that you've said it, you might as well finish."

"It's really nothing. It's just that I'd been kind of planning on having pretty rugs and . . ."

"*Planning* on having them!" interrupted Miss Polly, sharply.

Pollyanna blushed again, even more painfully. "I know I shouldn't have, Aunt Polly," she apologized. "I guess it's just that I've never had them. Of course, we did have two rugs that came in the missionary barrels. But they were little. One had ink spots, and the other had holes. And we never had more than two pictures. Fath—I mean, *we*—had to sell the good one, and the bad one broke. If it hadn't been for that, I wouldn't have wanted so much to have pretty things. And the first time I saw all those lovely rooms downstairs I shouldn't have started planning how pretty mine would be. But truly, Aunt Polly, it only took a minute—well, a few minutes—until I started feeling glad that I didn't have a mirror, because then I wouldn't see my freckles. And there couldn't be a picture any nicer than the one out my window. And you've been so good to me that . . ."

Miss Polly stood up abruptly. Her face was very red. "That's enough, Pollyanna," she said stiffly. And then she swept out of the room, having forgotten entirely about the white sweater.

Less than 24 hours later, Miss Polly said to Nancy, crisply, "You may move Miss Pollyanna's things downstairs this morning. I have decided that, for now, my niece will sleep in the room directly below the attic room."

"Yes, ma'am," Nancy said to Miss Polly. *Thank goodness!* she said to herself.

And a minute later, she exclaimed joyously to Pollyanna, "From now on, you're going to sleep in the room under this one. You really are!"

Pollyanna grew pale. "You mean it, Nancy? Really and truly?"

"Really and truly," Nancy answered, taking an armful of dresses out of the closet. "And I'm going to put all your things downstairs right away—before she has a chance to change her mind."

But before Nancy had finished her sentence, Pollyanna flew down the stairs, taking them two at a time. "Bang!" went one door. Then "bang!"

went another. And a chair crashed to the ground as Pollyanna charged toward her goal—Aunt Polly.

"Oh, Aunt Polly! Aunt Polly! Do you mean it? Really and truly? Why, that room has *everything*—the rugs and the curtains and three windows, too. And it even has the picture of the outside, since the windows face the same way. Oh, Aunt Polly!"

"Very well, Pollyanna," Miss Polly said sternly. Miss Polly didn't know why, but suddenly she felt like crying. She wasn't used to feeling that way. So she hardened her voice to keep from crying. "I am pleased, of course, that you like the change. I trust that since you like all those things, you will take proper care of them. Now please pick up that chair. And you have banged two doors in the last 30 seconds."

Pollyanna picked up the chair. "Yes, ma'am. I'm sorry I banged those doors," she explained cheerfully. "But if you'd just found out about the room, I'll bet you'd bang doors, too." Pollyanna stopped short and looked more closely at her aunt. "Aunt Polly, did *you* ever bang doors?"

"I should hope *not!*" Miss Polly's face looked properly shocked.

"Why, Aunt Polly, what a shame!" Pollyanna's face looked concerned and sympathetic.

"A *shame!*" repeated Aunt Polly, too dazed to say more.

"Why, yes. If you'd ever felt glad enough to bang doors, you would have banged them. You see, if you feel that way, you just can't help it. So if you never banged doors, then you were never that glad for anything. And I'm sorry you've never felt that glad!"

"*Pollyanna!*" gasped the lady. But Pollyanna had already gone to help Nancy bring down her things.

Miss Polly heard the distant bang of the attic door and felt vaguely disturbed. She had, after all, felt that glad—at one time in her life.

Chapter
11

Introducing Jimmy

Tugust came, and brought with it several surprises and changes. Indeed, ever since Pollyanna arrived, there had been quite a few surprises and changes in Miss Polly Harrington's household.

First there was the kitten.

Pollyanna found the kitten mewing pitifully in the middle of the road. She asked the neighbors if any of them owned the kitten. When no one claimed it, Pollyanna, of course, brought it home with her.

"And I was glad I didn't find anyone who owned it, too," Pollyanna admitted happily to her aunt. "I wanted so much to bring it home. I love kittens. And I knew you'd be glad to let it live here."

Miss Polly looked at the pathetic little gray bunch of matted, dirty fur in Pollyanna's arms and shivered. Miss Polly did not like cats—not even pretty, healthy, clean ones. "How awful, Pollyanna! What a dirty little beast! I'm sure it's sick, and all full of dirt and fleas."

"I know—the poor little thing," said Pollyanna, tenderly. She looked into the little creature's frightened eyes. "And it's trembling, too. It's so scared. You see, it doesn't know yet that we're going to keep it."

"It's not the only one who doesn't know that," said Miss Polly sternly.

"Oh, no," explained Pollyanna, not understanding what her aunt meant. "I told everybody that we'd keep it. I knew you'd be glad to take in such a poor, lonely, little thing!"

Miss Polly opened her lips and tried to speak. But it was no use. Once again she was feeling strangely helpless. It was a feeling she often had, ever since Pollyanna had arrived.

"I knew you'd feel that way," Pollyanna said, gratefully. "After all, you took *me* in. So I knew you wouldn't let a dear little lonely kitten go hunting for a home. And that's what I told Mrs. Ford when she asked if you'd let me keep it."

"But Pollyanna—Pollyanna . . ." protested Miss Polly, who hated cats. "I don't . . ."

But it was too late. Pollyanna was already running into the kitchen, calling, "Nancy! Nancy! Look at this dear little kitten that Aunt Polly is going to bring up along with me!"

The next day, Pollyanna brought home a dog. She assumed that Miss Polly would want also to protect this poor animal, which was even dirtier and more pathetic than the kitten. But Miss Polly hated dogs even more than cats, if that were possible. Yet the woman was so amazed that Pollyanna thought of her as an angel of mercy that she again felt helpless to protest.

A few days later, Pollyanna brought home a small, ragged boy. She was sure that her aunt would take him in, too. But that's when Miss Polly finally said something. This is how it happened.

That Thursday morning, Pollyanna was coming back from seeing Mrs. Snow. She and Pollyanna had become the best of friends. Mrs. Snow was even playing the game now—though not very well. She had been feeling sorry about everything for such a long time. So it wasn't easy anymore to be glad for anything. But with Pollyanna's cheerful help, she was learning fast. Today, to Pollyanna's huge delight, Mrs. Snow said she was glad that Pollyanna brought her ham because that was just what she had been wanting. But Milly later told Pollyanna that, in fact, Mrs. Snow had already been given a plate of ham that day.

Pollyanna was thinking about this when suddenly she saw the boy. He was sitting at the edge of the road, half-heartedly carving a small stick with a dull, broken-bladed knife.

"Hello," Pollyanna greeted him, smiling.

The boy glanced up, then looked away.

"Hello, yourself," he mumbled.

Pollyanna laughed. "You don't look like you'd be glad even about a plate of ham," she chuckled and sat down beside him. She bravely said that she really didn't mind being with adults all the time. But sometimes she longed for friends her own age.

"My name's Pollyanna Whittier," she began. "What's yours?"

"Jimmy Bean," he grunted, as if he didn't care. He glanced quickly at Pollyanna and then looked away.

"Good! Now we're introduced. I'm glad you did your part. Some folks don't, you know. I live at Miss Polly Harrington's house. Where do you live?"

"Nowhere."

"Nowhere! Why, you can't do that! Everybody lives somewhere!"

"Well, I don't, silly. At least, not right now. I'm looking for a new place."

Pollyanna did not like to be called "silly." Still, he was someone to talk to who wasn't a grownup.

"Where did you live before?" she asked.

"You sure do ask a lot of questions," the boy muttered.

"That's because I have to. If you'd talk more, I could talk less."

The boy gave an embarrassed little laugh. Then he finally turned toward Pollyanna. "All right then. Here goes! I'm Jimmy Bean, and I'm ten years old. I came here last year to live at the Orphans' Home. But they've got so many kids that there isn't room for me. And I don't think they ever really wanted me, anyway. So I decided to live somewhere else. I just haven't found the place, yet. Sure, I'd *like* a home—just an ordinary home with a mother in it, instead of a director. If it's a home, then it's your family. And I haven't had any family since—since my dad died." The boy paused to steady his voice. Then he continued, "So I'm looking for a new place. I've already tried four houses. But they didn't want me—even though I said I'd work for them. There! Does that answer your questions?"

"Oh, dear! I know just how you feel. After—after my father died, nobody but the Ladies' Aid wanted me. But then Aunt Polly said she'd take . . ." Pollyanna stopped abruptly. "Oh, I know just the place for you! Aunt Polly will take you. I know she will! After all, she took me. And she took Fluffy and Buffy, when they didn't have anyone to love them or anyplace to go. And they're only a cat and a dog. Oh, Aunt Polly's so good and kind. I just know she'll take you, too!"

Jimmy Bean's thin little face brightened. "Really? I'd work for her, you know. And I'm real strong!" He showed her a small, bony arm.

"Of course she will! Why, my Aunt Polly is the nicest lady in the world. And there are lots of rooms in the house." Pollyanna jumped up and tugged his arm. But then she added, as they hurried away, "Of course, you might have to sleep in the attic room at first. I did. But now there are screens, so it won't be so hot. And the flies won't get in with the germ things on their feet. Why, maybe Aunt Polly will let you read the book about the flies if you're good—I mean, if you're bad. And since you've got freckles, too, you'll be glad there aren't any mirrors. And the outdoor picture is so much nicer than any . . ." Pollyanna panted, suddenly out of breath.

"Golly!" Jimmy Bean exclaimed admiringly. "You sure can talk a lot—even when you're running. I'll bet you could fill the time yourself, without asking so many questions!"

Pollyanna laughed. "Well then, you can be glad that while I'm talking, *you* don't have to!"

As soon as they reached the house, Pollyanna presented Jimmy to her amazed aunt.

"Just look, Aunt Polly!" she exclaimed triumphantly. "I've brought you something to bring up that's even nicer than Fluffy or Buffy. It's a real live boy! He won't mind a bit if he has to sleep in the attic at first. And he says he'll work. But I'll need him most of the time to play with."

Miss Polly's face first grew pale. Then it darkened. "Pollyanna, who is this dirty little boy? Where did you find him?" she demanded sharply.

Jimmy looked nervously at the door. But Pollyanna laughed merrily. "He is dirty—but so were Fluffy and Buffy when you took them in. And I'll bet washing will improve him, too. But now I'm being as rude as the Man—forgetting about proper introductions. Aunt Polly, this is Jimmy Bean."

"Well, what is he doing here?"

"Why, he's for you, Aunt Polly. I brought him home so he could live here. He wants a home and family. I told him how good you were to me—and to Fluffy and Buffy. And that I know you'll be good to him, too, because he's even nicer than cats and dogs."

Miss Polly gasped, once again feeling strangely helpless. Finally she said firmly, "That will do, Pollyanna. This is the craziest thing you've done yet. Stray cats and mangy dogs are bad enough. But now you want to bring home ragged little street beggars who . . ."

Suddenly the boy stepped right up to Miss Polly. His chin held high and his eyes flashing, he protested fearlessly, "I ain't a beggar, ma'am. And I don't want nothing from you. I figured I'd work for my room and board. And I'd never have come to your old house except that this girl made me. She kept telling me how you're so good and so kind that you'd be dying to take me in. So there!" he said, as he turned and stormed out of the room.

"Oh, Aunt Polly!" Pollyanna cried. "Why, I thought you'd be *glad* to have him here."

Miss Polly's nerves snapped at last. "Pollyanna!" she exploded. "You *must* stop using that infernal word 'glad'! All that 'glad,' 'glad,' 'glad' from morning till night is driving me crazy!"

Pollyanna's jaw dropped in shock. Finally she gasped, "Why, Aunt Polly. I thought you'd be glad that I was so gl— Oh!" Pollyanna clapped her hand to her mouth and rushed out of the room.

Pollyanna caught up with the boy before he'd reached the end of the driveway. "Jimmy Bean! Jimmy Bean!" she called, panting. "I'm so sorry!"

"Forget it. I ain't blaming you," he answered, angrily. "But I ain't no beggar, neither!" he added, lifting his chin.

"Of course you aren't! But don't blame Aunt Polly," she pleaded. "I probably didn't introduce you properly. She's good and kind. Really she is, and always has been, too. Oh, I do wish I could find a place for you!"

"Never mind," the boy said, shrugging his shoulders and turning away. "I guess I can find one myself. I ain't no beggar, you know."

Pollyanna frowned and thought for a while. Suddenly she said brightly, "I know what I'll do! The Ladies' Aid meets this afternoon. I'll tell them all about you and ask them to help. That's what Father always did when he needed something—medicine for sick people or new rugs or whatever."

"Well, I ain't a sick person or a rug," the boy said, indignantly. "Besides, what is a Ladies' Aid anyway?"

"Why, Jimmy Bean! Where were you brought up?" Pollyanna said, shocked by his ignorance.

"Well, never mind, if you ain't telling," the boy grunted, starting to walk away.

Pollyanna ran to his side. "Why, it's just a lot of ladies that meet and sew and raise money and talk. They're awfully kind—at least, most of mine were, back home. I'm going to tell them about you this afternoon."

"Oh no, you won't!" he said fiercely. "I'm not going to stand around and hear a whole *lot* of women call me a beggar. *One* was bad enough!"

"Oh, but you wouldn't be there," Pollyanna explained. "I'd go alone, of course, and tell them."

"You would?"

"Yes. And I'd tell it better this time. And some of them, I'm sure, would be glad to give you a home."

"Don't forget to tell them I'll work."

"I won't," Pollyanna promised. "Meet me tomorrow where I found you today, and I'll tell you what they say."

"All right. I'll be there. But maybe I'd better go back to the Home for tonight. You see, I don't have no other place to stay. But they're not like *family*, you know. They don't *care!*"

"I know," Pollyanna nodded, understanding how he felt. "But I'm sure that when I see you tomorrow I'll have a normal home for you and people that really care. "Goodbye!" she called cheerfully, as she turned back toward the house.

From the living room window, Miss Polly watched the two children. She sighed. In her ears she heard the girl's words about her being "so good and kind." But in her heart, she felt a strange sense of emptiness—a sense of loss.

Chapter 12

Before the Ladies' Aid

Lunch, which was always served promptly at noon, was a silent meal that day. Pollyanna tried to talk. But she had to keep cutting off her sentences each time she started to use the word "glad."

The fifth time this happened, Miss Polly sighed wearily, "There, there child. Say it if you want to. It would be better than making all this fuss."

"Oh, thank you," Pollyanna said, her worried face brightening. "It's hard not to say it. You see, I've played it so long."

"You've—what?" demanded Aunt Polly.

"Played it. The game, you know, that Father . . ." Pollyanna stopped with a painful blush. Once again she found herself unintentionally saying a forbidden word.

Aunt Polly frowned and said nothing. The rest of the meal was silent.

A little later, Pollyanna heard Aunt Polly phone the minister's wife to say she would not be at the Ladies' Aid meeting that afternoon. She had a headache and was going to lie down. Pollyanna tried to feel sorry about the headache. But she couldn't help feeling glad that her aunt would not be there when she presented Jimmy Bean's case to the Ladies' Aid. She did not want her aunt to tell them he was a "ragged little street beggar."

Pollyanna decided to wait until she was sure that all the Ladies' Aiders would have arrived. So she arrived at the church a little before three o'clock. Bravely, and with quiet confidence, Pollyanna pushed open the door. The chatter and laughter turned to a surprised hush. Pollyanna stepped forward a little timidly. After all, these women were still mostly strangers to her—not the same dear Ladies' Aiders she had known out West.

"How do you do, Ladies' Aiders?" Pollyanna began hesitantly. "I'm Pollyanna Whittier. I guess some of you may know who I am."

There was an embarrassed silence. Some of the ladies had already met this rather extraordinary child. Nearly all had heard stories about her. But not one could think of anything to say.

"I—I've come to—to lay the case before you,"

Pollyanna stammered. This was what her father used to say. There was a slight rustle.

"Did your aunt send you, my dear?" the minister's wife asked.

Pollyanna blushed. "Oh, no. I came all by myself. I'm used to Ladies' Aiders. They brought me up, you see—with Father."

One of the ladies started whispering loudly.

The minister's wife frowned. "Yes, dear. What is it, then?"

"Well, it's Jimmy Bean," Pollyanna sighed. "The only home he has is the Orphans' one. And they're full and don't really want him. So Jimmy wants an ordinary home, the kind with a mother or a father instead of a director in it. You know, a family that will care about him. He's ten years old going on eleven. So I thought some of you might want him to live with you."

"Well, I never—!" a voice gasped, finally breaking the shocked silence.

With worried eyes, Pollyanna looked at all the stern faces around her. Then she added eagerly, "Oh, I almost forgot to tell you. He will work, too."

There was a cold silence.

Finally the women started talking among themselves.

Pollyanna could not understand everything they were saying. But they did not sound very happy. Each woman seemed to think that someone else could offer Jimmy a home. But no one agreed to take him herself. Then the minister's wife suggested that they could spend some of their money to support Jimmy Bean's care and education, instead of sending quite so much to support little boys in faraway India.

Then the talking grew louder and angrier than before. Some of the ladies argued that they would die of embarrassment if the name of their Ladies' Aid Society wasn't at the top of the list of contributors in a certain report. The ladies finally decided that they should send all their money to bring up little boys in India rather than spend a little of it to bring up one little boy in their own town. It seemed the only way for them to get "credit in the report."

Pollyanna was glad when she could finally leave that unpleasant discussion. But she was very sorry that she'd have to tell Jimmy Bean about their decision. *They acted as if little boys here didn't matter at all—only little boys far away,* Pollyanna sighed. *But why would they want see their name on a report rather than see a little boy grow up happy?*

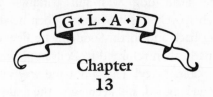

In Pendleton Woods

It had been a hard day, and Pollyanna didn't have to be home until 5:30. So she decided to take a peaceful walk through the green quiet of Pendleton Woods. Today Pollyanna found the beautiful woods even more delightful than usual. She looked up at the patches of vivid blue between the sunlit treetops and sighed. "If only those ladies who talked so loud could come up here. I bet they'd change their minds and take in Jimmy Bean."

Suddenly Pollyanna heard a dog bark. A moment later it came dashing toward her, still barking.

Pollyanna recognized the dog. She'd seen him with the Man, Mr. John Pendleton. Pollyanna looked down the path, hoping to see Mr. Pendleton. But he never appeared. So Pollyanna continued walking along the path.

The little dog was still barking—giving short, sharp yelps, as if of alarm. Then he started running back and forth. Suddenly he flew down a side path, then returned to Pollyanna, whining and barking. "Hey! That's not the way home," Pollyanna laughed, still keeping to the main path.

By now the little dog seemed frantic. He kept dashing back and forth, back and forth between Pollyanna and the side path, barking and whining pitifully. His little brown body quivered, and his brown eyes pleaded with Pollyanna. At last she understood, turned, and followed him.

Now the little dog raced madly down the path. Before long, Pollyanna saw why. At the foot of a steep cliff, a few yards from the path, a man lay motionless. When he heard Pollyanna's footsteps, the man turned his head.

With a startled cry, Pollyanna ran to his side. "Mr. Pendleton! Are you hurt?"

"Hurt? Oh, no!" the man snapped sarcastically. "I'm just taking a little nap in the sunshine! Of course, I'm hurt! See here. What do you know? What can you do? Can you follow instructions?"

"Well, I guess I don't know very much, and I can't do a lot. But most of the Ladies' Aiders back home said I could follow instructions, although Mrs. Rawson used to say . . ."

The man interrupted her. "There, there, child. I'm sorry. It's just that this darned leg of mine. . . . Now listen." He reached, with difficulty, into his pocket and brought out a bunch of keys. Holding one key between his thumb and finger, he explained. "Straight through the path over there, about five minutes from here, is my house. Use this key to enter the side door. Then go through the hall and into the room at the back of the house. There you'll find a telephone. Do you know how to use a telephone?"

"Oh, yes, sir! Why, once when Aunt Polly . . ."

"Never mind your Aunt Polly!" the man interrupted angrily. "You'll find a list of phone numbers somewhere near the phone. Look up Dr. Thomas Chilton's number. Tell him that John Pendleton is at the foot of Little Eagle Ledge in Pendleton Woods with a broken leg. Tell him to come right away with a stretcher and two men. He'll know what else to do."

"A broken leg? Oh, Mr. Pendleton! How perfectly awful!" Pollyanna shuddered. "But I'm so glad I came! I wish I could do . . ."

"But you're not. Now will you go and do what I said, and stop talking," the man moaned, in great pain.

With a little sob, Pollyanna hurried away. She did not stop now to look up at the patches of blue between the sunlit treetops. Instead, she kept her eyes on the ground, trying to run as quickly as she could.

Soon she saw the house. It was so big and gray that she was almost frightened to go inside.

But she ran across the neglected lawn and tried the key in the lock. At last the heavy wooden door swung open.

Pollyanna caught her breath. The house was dark and gloomy. It was a house of mystery, which no one but Mr. Pendleton was allowed to enter. She'd even heard that somewhere in the house was a skeleton!

Looking neither to the right nor the left, Pollyanna raced down the hall and opened another door. In the middle of the dreary, dusty room, she saw a large, untidy desk with the telephone on it. The list of phone numbers had fallen to the floor. But Pollyanna found it. With a shaking hand, she dialed Dr. Chilton's number, delivered her message, and hung up the phone with relief.

In what seemed to the injured man an incredibly short time, Pollyanna was back at his side.

"Well, what happened? Couldn't you get in?" he demanded.

"Why, of course I could!" Pollyanna answered in surprise. "I wouldn't be here if I hadn't gotten in! And the doctor knew just where you were, so I didn't stay to show him. I wanted to be with you."

"You did?" the man smiled grimly. "I should think you might be able to find pleasanter people to be with!"

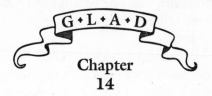

Just a Matter of Ham

When Pollyanna finally got home, Nancy met her at the door. "Well, I sure am glad to see you!" she exclaimed in relief. "I was getting worried about you. It's already 6:30!"

"I know I'm late for dinner," Pollyanna said anxiously. "But it's not my fault—really it's not. And I don't think even Aunt Polly will say it is."

"Well, don't worry. She won't be able to. She's gone."

"Gone!" gasped Pollyanna. She felt a sharp pang of guilt for bringing home things that seemed to upset her aunt—a stray cat, a mangy dog, a ragged boy, the unwelcome "glad," and the forbidden "father." "Oh, Nancy," Pollyanna cried. "You think that *I* drove her away?"

"Of course not!" Nancy snorted. "Her cousin in Boston died suddenly. She had to go there for the funeral and won't be back for three days. So I guess we can be real glad it'll be just you and me all that time!"

Pollyanna looked shocked. "Glad! Oh, Nancy! How can we be glad when it's a funeral?"

"Oh, I wasn't glad for the *funeral,* Miss Pollyanna! I was glad because . . ." Nancy stopped abruptly. "Why, Miss Pollyanna, it was *you* who taught me to play the game."

Pollyanna frowned. "I know, Nancy. But it doesn't seem right to play the game about some things. I can't help thinking that there's nothing in a funeral to be glad for."

Nancy chuckled. "Well, we can at least be glad that it isn't ours," she said quietly.

But Pollyanna didn't hear her. She rushed to tell Nancy all about the accident. And soon Nancy was listening, wide-eyed.

The next afternoon, Pollyanna and Jimmy Bean met as they had planned. Of course, Jimmy was bitterly disappointed that the Ladies' Aid liked little boys from India more than him.

"Well, maybe it's natural," Jimmy sighed. "You know how the potato on somebody else's plate always looks bigger than the one on your own? Well, I wished I looked that way to somebody far away. Wouldn't it be just great if somebody over in India wanted *me?*"

Pollyanna clapped her hands. "Why, of course! That's the very thing, Jimmy! I'll write to my own Ladies' Aiders about you. They aren't over in India. They're only out West. But that's really far away, just the same."

Jimmy's face brightened. "Do you think they really would take me?" he asked.

"Of course they will! Why, they can just pretend that you're a little boy from India. I bet you you're far enough away to get their names into a report. You'll see. I'll write Mrs. White. No, I'll write Mrs. Jones. Mrs. White has the most money. But Mrs. Jones gives the most. When you think about it, that's kind of funny, isn't it?"

"All right. But don't forget to say I'll work for my room and board. I ain't no beggar. And business is business—even with Ladies' Aiders." He hesitated. "So I guess I'd better stay where I am until you hear?"

"Of course. That way I'll know where to find you. And I'm sure they'll take you. Just like Aunt Polly took me." Pollyanna thought a moment. "Do you think that I was Aunt Polly's little girl from India?"

The next week, Pollyanna asked her aunt, "Would you mind very much if this week I took Mrs. Snow's ham to someone else? I'm sure Mrs. Snow wouldn't mind—just this once."

"Dear me, Pollyanna! What are you up to now?" sighed her aunt. "You certainly are a most extraordinary child!"

Pollyanna frowned, worried. "Aunt Polly, what does 'extraordinary' mean? If you're 'extraordinary,' then you can't be 'ordinary,' can you?"

"Certainly not."

"Well, then, I'm glad I'm 'extraordinary.' You see, Mrs. White used to say that Mrs. Rawson was a very ordinary woman. And she hated Mrs. Rawson. Fath—I mean, we had trouble keeping those two Ladies' Aiders from fight . . ."

"Yes, yes. Well, never mind," Aunt Polly said impatiently. "You do run on so, Pollyanna. And no matter what we're talking about, you always bring up those Ladies' Aiders!"

"Yes'm," Pollyanna smiled cheerfully. "I guess maybe I do. But that's because they used to bring *me* up, and . . ."

"That will do, Pollyanna," her aunt interrupted coldly. "Now, what is it about this ham?"

"Nothing, really, that you would mind, I'm sure. After all, you let me take ham to her. So I thought you wouldn't mind my taking some to *him*. I mean, a broken leg won't last forever, like Mrs. Snow's illness. So after just once or twice, all the rest can go to her."

"'Him'? 'Broken leg'? What are you talking about, Pollyanna?"

"Oh, I forgot you didn't know. You see, it happened the day you left. That's when I found him in the woods, and had to unlock his house, and telephone for the doctor and the men, and hold his head. And I haven't seen him since. So when Nancy made the ham for Mrs. Snow this week, I thought how nice it would be if I could take it to him instead of her—just this once. Aunt Polly, may I?"

"Yes, yes. I suppose so," agreed Miss Polly, wearily. "Now who did you say he was?"

"Mr. John Pendleton."

Miss Polly almost jumped out of her chair. *"John Pendleton!"*

"Yes. Maybe you know him?"

Miss Polly, instead of answering, asked, "Do *you* know him?"

Pollyanna nodded. "Oh, yes. He always speaks and smiles—now. He's only cranky on the outside, you know. I guess I'll go and get the ham, then."

"Pollyanna, wait!" Miss Polly said sternly. "I've changed my mind. I would prefer that Mrs. Snow have the ham, as usual. That is all. You may go now."

Pollyanna's face fell. "But Aunt Polly. Mrs. Snow's problem will last. She can always be sick and have things wrong with her. But he's only got a broken leg, and legs don't last—broken ones, I mean. He's had it a whole week already."

"But I do not care to send ham to John Pendleton, Pollyanna," Miss Polly said stiffly.

"I know he's cranky on the outside," Pollyanna admitted sadly. "So I can see why you don't like him. But I wouldn't say the ham was from you. I'd say it was from me. I like him. I'd be glad to send him ham."

Miss Polly shook her head again. Then she asked, in a strangely quiet voice, "Does he know who you are, Pollyanna?"

The little girl sighed. "I guess not. Once I introduced myself, but he never calls me by my name. Never."

"Does he know where you live?"

"Oh, no. I never told him that."

"Then he doesn't know you're my niece?"

"I don't think so."

For a moment there was silence. Miss Polly was looking at Pollyanna, but without really seeing her at all. After thinking for a while, Miss Polly finally said in a voice that was unusually quiet for her, "Very well, Pollyanna. You may take the ham to Mr. Pendleton as your own gift. But be very sure he does not think that I am the one who sent it."

"Yes'm—no'm—I mean, thank you, Aunt Polly!" exclaimed Pollyanna joyfully, as she flew through the door.

Dr. Chilton

The second time she went to Mr. John Pendleton's house, Pollyanna noticed that the big, gray house looked very different. Windows were open, an elderly woman was hanging clothes in the back yard, and the doctor's carriage was parked in the driveway.

As before, Pollyanna went to the side door. But this time she rang the doorbell.

The little dog ran up the steps to greet her. When the woman opened the door, Pollyanna said, smiling, "I've brought some ham for Mr. Pendleton."

"Thank you," said the woman, reaching for the plate in the little girl's hand. "I'd be happy to take it to him. Who shall I say sent it?"

Just then the doctor walked into the hall. He heard the woman's words and saw the disappointed look on Pollyanna's face. "Ham? Why, that would be fine for Mr. Pendleton. Maybe you'd like to see our patient?" he asked Pollyanna.

"Oh, yes, sir," Pollyanna beamed.

The woman, surprised, led the way to Mr. Pendleton's room.

In the hallway, the nurse who was caring for the patient protested as he said, "But, Doctor. Didn't Mr. Pendleton give orders not to admit anyone?"

"Oh, yes," the doctor nodded calmly. "But I'm giving orders now. That little girl will cure him better than six boxes of pills. If anything or anybody can make Pendleton feel better, she can. That's why I sent her in."

"Who is she?"

The doctor hesitated for a moment, then answered, "She's the niece of one of our best known citizens. I haven't yet had the pleasure of getting to know the little lady personally. But I'm thankful that lots of my patients have."

The nurse smiled. "And what are the special ingredients of her wonder-working medicine?"

The doctor shook his head. "I don't know. As nearly as I can tell, it's an unstoppable, indestructible gladness for everything that has happened or is going to happen. My patients are constantly repeating her little speeches. And the gist of most of them is 'just being glad.' I wish I could prescribe her, the way I'd prescribe pills. Of course, if there were too many Pollyannas in this

world, you and I would soon be out of business!"
he said laughing, as he left the house.

Meanwhile, Pollyanna, on her way to Mr.
Pendleton's room, noticed many changes from
her first visit. There was no trash on the floor, no
clutter on the desk, and not even a speck of dust
in sight.

When they reached the bedroom, the maid
said in a frightened voice, "If you please, sir.
Here's a little girl with some ham. The doctor
said I was to bring her in."

The next moment, Pollyanna found herself
alone with a very grumpy-looking man, who was
lying flat on his back in bed.

"See here. Didn't I say . . ." he began angrily.
But when Pollyanna stepped closer to the bed he
said, rather coldly, "Oh, it's you."

"Yes, sir," smiled Pollyanna. "Oh, I'm so glad
they let me in! You see, at first the lady almost
took my plate. And I was so afraid I wasn't going
to see you at all. Then the doctor came, and
he said I could. Wasn't he lovely to let me see
you?"

In spite of himself, the man's lips twitched
into a smile. But all he said was, "Humph!"

"And I've brought you some of Nancy's
homemade ham," Pollyanna continued. "I hope
you like it?"

The smile turned to a frown. "Never had it
before."

For a brief instant, Pollyanna looked disappointed. But then she brightened as she set down the plate of ham. "You haven't? Well, then, if you haven't, then you can't know that you *don't* like it, anyhow. So I guess I'm glad you haven't, after all. Now if you knew . . ."

"Yes, yes. Well, there's one thing I do know, all right. And that is I'm flat on my back right now and I'll probably stay like this forever."

Pollyanna looked shocked. "Oh, no! You couldn't stay like that forever! If you did, why you'd start to smell and become all rotten and—not that I think you could ever be rotten—it's just that, well, on the *outside* you might—that is, if you stayed like that forever—not that I wouldn't want you to live forever, even if you had to stay like that—only I just thought that if . . ."

Suddenly John Pendleton started laughing out loud. The nurse, startled by the sound, looked in the room. But like a cook who opens an oven door to check on a half-done cake, he quickly shut the door again before the cold air could stop the cake from rising.

"Aren't you getting a little mixed-up?" John Pendleton asked Pollyanna between chuckles.

The little girl laughed. "Maybe. But what I mean is that legs don't last—broken ones, that is. Not like Mrs. Snow's illness. So yours won't last forever. I should think you could be glad of that."

"Oh, sure I am," the man muttered grimly.

"And you broke only one leg. You can be glad you didn't break two," Pollyanna added enthusiastically.

"Oh, sure! How lucky I am!" the man said sharply. "Looking at things that way, I guess I should be glad that I'm not a centipede and didn't break *fifty* of my hundred legs!"

Pollyanna chuckled. "Oh, that's the best one yet! And you can also be glad . . ."

"Of course," the man interrupted, the old bitterness coming back to his voice. "I suppose I can be glad, too, for the nurse and the doctor and that darn woman in the kitchen!"

"Why, yes, sir. Just think how bad it would be if you *didn't* have them!"

"What?" he demanded sharply.

"I'm just saying, think how bad it would be if you didn't have them—with you lying here like this!"

"But that's the very thing that's causing all this trouble—the fact that I'm lying here like this! And yet, you expect me to say I'm *glad* because some fool woman disrupts the whole house and calls it 'organizing.' And because some bossy man pokes me and orders me around and calls it 'nursing.' Not to mention the doctor who eggs them on. And the whole bunch of them expecting me to pay them for all this trouble—and pay them well, too!"

Pollyanna frowned sympathetically. "Yes, I know. *That* part really is too bad—about the money—when you've been saving it all this time."

"When I've been what?"

"Saving money. Buying only things that are cheap."

"Look here, child. What are you talking about?"

Pollyanna smiled brightly. "Why, about your money. You know. Instead of spending money on yourself, you save it to give to charities. That's one way I knew that you weren't cranky inside. You see, I found out about it—from Nancy."

The man's jaw dropped in surprise. "Nancy told you I was saving money to give to—Well, then. May I ask who Nancy is?"

"Our Nancy. She works for Aunt Polly."

"Aunt Polly! And just who is Aunt Polly?"

"She's Miss Polly Harrington. I live with her."

The man made a sudden movement. "Miss Polly Harrington!" he gasped. "You live with *her*?"

"Yes. I'm her niece. She's taken me in to bring me up—you know, because of my mother," Pollyanna said quietly. "They were sisters. And after Father . . ." Pollyanna's voice broke for a moment. Then she continued, "Well, there wasn't anyone left to take care of me except for the Ladies' Aid. So Aunt Polly took me."

The man did not answer. His face was very pale—so pale that Pollyanna was frightened. She stood up, uncertain what to do.

"I guess maybe I'd better go now," she suggested. "I hope you like the ham."

The man turned his head and gazed at Pollyanna. The look in his eyes was suddenly warm and caring.

"And so, you are—you are Miss Polly Harrington's niece," he said gently, his dark eyes lingering on her face.

"Yes, sir. I suppose you know her?"

John Pendleton's lips curved in an odd smile. "Oh, yes. I know her." He hesitated, and then went on. "But, you don't mean—you *can't* mean—that it was Miss Polly Harrington who sent that ham to me?"

"Oh, no, sir," Pollyanna said, looking upset. "*She* didn't. And she said to be sure you didn't think so. But I . . ."

"I thought as much," the man muttered, turning his head.

So Pollyanna, even more upset, tiptoed from the room.

In front of the house, she saw the doctor waiting in his carriage. "Well, Miss Pollyanna, may I have the pleasure of driving you home?" the doctor asked, smiling.

"Oh thank you, sir. I just love going for rides," she beamed.

"Do you?" the doctor smiled. "Well, as nearly as I can tell, there are lots of things you 'love' doing."

Pollyanna laughed. "Well, I don't know. I guess maybe there are," she admitted. "I like to do almost everything that's *living*. But of course there are some things I don't like very much— like sewing and reading out loud. But they aren't *living*."

"No? Well, what are they, then?"

"Aunt Polly says they're 'learning to live,'" sighed Pollyanna.

"Does she?" he asked, with a sad little smile. "Well, I guess I shouldn't be surprised she'd say that."

"But I don't see things that way at all," Pollyanna explained. "I don't think you have to *learn* how to live. I didn't, anyway."

The doctor gave a heavy sigh. "Well, I'm afraid some of us do have to."

Pollyanna, glancing at his face, suddenly felt sorry for him. He looked so sad. She wished that she could do something to make him feel better. Finally she said, timidly, "Dr. Chilton, I should think that being a doctor would be the very gladdest kind of job anyone could have."

"'Gladdest'!" the doctor exclaimed in surprise. "When I see so much suffering—all the time, everywhere I go?"

Pollyanna nodded. "I know. But you're *helping* it! Don't you see? And, of course, you're glad to help it! And so that makes you the gladdest of any of us."

The doctor's eyes suddenly filled with tears. He had a lonely life. He had no wife and no home except for his two-room office in a boarding house. But his profession had always been very dear to him.

Looking into Pollyanna's shining eyes, he felt as if a loving hand had suddenly been placed on his head. No matter how long the day or weary the night, that radiant look in Pollyanna's eyes would continue to bless his work and remind him of his noble calling.

"Thank you, little girl," he said, his voice cracking. Then, with the bright smile his patients knew and loved, he added, "Now I'm thinking that it was the doctor, as much as his patient, who needed some of that special 'medicine'!"

The doctor drove Pollyanna to her front door, smiled at Nancy, and then drove rapidly away.

"I've had a perfectly beautiful ride with the doctor," Pollyanna announced, running up the steps. "He's lovely, Nancy!"

"Is he?"

"Yes. And I told him I thought his job must be the very gladdest one there was."

"What? Going to see sick people? And people that aren't sick, but think they are—which is even worse." Nancy looked doubtful.

Pollyanna laughed cheerfully. "That's pretty much what he said, too. But there's a way to be glad even then. Guess!"

Nancy frowned, thinking over the problem. She was beginning to enjoy playing this game of "being glad."

Finally she said, chuckling, "Oh, I know. It's just the opposite of what you told Mrs. Snow."

"Opposite?"

"Yes. You told her she could be glad because other people weren't sick like her. Well, the doctor can be glad because he isn't sick like the patients he treats!" Nancy said, triumphantly.

Now it was Pollyanna who frowned. "Why, yes," she admitted. "I guess that's one way to look at it. But it isn't the way I said. And besides, I somehow don't quite like how that one sounds. He wouldn't be glad that his patients are sick, but that . . .Oh, sometimes you do play the game in a funny way, Nancy."

Pollyanna sighed and went into the house. There she found her aunt in the living room.

"Who was that man, Pollyanna?" the lady asked, a little sharply. "The one who drove up to the house?"

"Why, Aunt Polly! That was Dr. Chilton. Don't you know him?"

"Dr. Chilton! What was he doing here?"

"He drove me home. Oh, and I gave the ham to Mr. Pendleton, and . . ."

Miss Polly looked up quickly. "Pollyanna, he did not think that I sent it?"

"Oh, no, Aunt Polly. I told him you didn't."

Suddenly Miss Polly blushed deeply. "You *told* him I didn't!"

Pollyanna's eyes widened—surprised and upset that her aunt seemed to be scolding her. "Why, Aunt Polly, you *said* to!"

Aunt Polly sighed. "I *said*, Pollyanna, that you were to be sure he did not think that I sent it. That is very different from telling him outright that I did not send it.

"Dear me! Well, I don't see what the difference is," sighed Pollyanna, as she hung her hat on the one particular hook where Aunt Polly said it must be hung.

Chapter 16

A Red Rose and a Lace Shawl

One rainy day the following week, Miss Polly returned from a meeting of the Ladies' Aid Society. During the ride home, the damp wind had blown her hair into dark curls and turned her cheeks a bright, pretty pink.

Pollyanna had never before seen Aunt Polly's hair down. "Oh! Oh! Oh!" Pollyanna exclaimed joyfully, as she danced around her aunt. "I never knew you had curls! Do you think someday I might, too? Of course, they wouldn't be black even if I did get them."

"Pollyanna, what does all this mean?" demanded Aunt Polly, quickly taking off her hat and trying to smooth back her hair.

"No, no! Please, Aunt Polly!" Pollyanna pleaded anxiously. "Don't smooth out those darling little black curls. Oh, Aunt Polly! They're so pretty!"

"Nonsense! And what do you mean, Pollyanna, by going to the Ladies' Aid and making a fuss about that beggar boy?"

"But it isn't nonsense," urged Pollyanna, too excited about her aunt's hair to pay attention to her question. "You don't know how pretty you look with your hair like that! Oh, Aunt Polly! Can't I please do your hair like I did Mrs. Snow's, and put in a flower, too? I'd so love to see you that way! Why, you'd be even prettier than she was!"

"Pollyanna!" Miss Polly said sharply—as if to cover up the joy Pollyanna's words had given her. After all, when was the last time that anybody cared how she looked? "Pollyanna, you did not answer my question. What gave you the foolish idea of going to the Ladies' Aid?"

"Yes'm, I know. But I didn't know it was foolish until I went and found out they'd rather see their report grow than see Jimmy grow. So then I wrote to *my* Ladies' Aiders because Jimmy is far away from them. And I thought maybe he could be like their little boy from India, just like— Aunt Polly, was I your little girl from India? And Aunt Polly, *will* you let me do your hair, please?"

Aunt Polly once again had that feeling of helplessness. "But Pollyanna, when the ladies told me this afternoon how you came to them, I felt so ashamed. I . . ."

Pollyanna began lightly dancing up and down on her toes. "You didn't! You didn't say I *couldn't* do your hair! So you meant it the other way around, sort of—like you didn't want me to say you didn't send the ham to Mr. Pendleton. Now wait just where you are. I'll get a comb."

"But Pollyanna," Aunt Polly protested, following her up to her own room.

"Oh, it'll be even nicer in here! Now sit down, please, right there. Oh, I'm so glad you let me do it!"

"But Pollyanna, I . . ."

Then, to her helpless amazement, Miss Pollyanna soon found herself sitting in front of her dressing table. Her hair was already tumbling around her ears. And ten eager, but very gentle fingers, were already at work.

"Oh, what pretty hair you've got!" chattered Pollyanna. "I'll bet people will be glad when they see it. And they'll be surprised, too, because you've hid it for so long. Why, Aunt Polly, I'll make you so pretty that everybody will just love to look at you!"

"Pollyanna!" Miss Polly gasped in shock. "I don't know why I'm letting you do such a silly thing."

"But Aunt Polly, I should think you'd be glad to have people like looking at you! Don't you like to look at pretty things? That always makes me feel happy."

"But . . . but . . ."

"And I *so* love doing people's hair. Oh, I just thought of something! But it's a surprise. So I have to leave you for a just a minute. But you must promise, promise, *promise* not to peek!" With that, Pollyanna ran from the room.

Miss Polly was already planning to undo her niece's foolish hairdo and put up her hair properly. As for "peeking," she really couldn't care less how—

But just then, Miss Polly happened to see herself in the dressing table mirror. She blushed. It was a face—no longer young—but bright with surprise and excitement. The hair lay in loose waves that flattered her face, with softening little curls here and there. Miss Polly was so amazed by the face in the mirror that she forgot about redoing her hair.

Pollyanna ran back into the room and slipped a blindfold over her aunt's eyes.

"Pollyanna! Pollyanna! What *are* you doing?" Miss Polly cried out.

Pollyanna chuckled. With trembling fingers, she draped across her aunt's shoulders a beautiful lace shawl that she'd found in the attic.

Pollyanna looked over her work with satisfaction. But then she thought of the perfect finishing touch. So she led her aunt to the sunroom. There she plucked a red rose and tucked it into the soft hair above Miss Polly's left ear.

"There!" she shouted, taking off the blindfold. "Oh, Aunt Polly! Now I guess you'll be glad I dressed you up!"

For one dazed moment, Miss Polly looked at her decorated self. Then she glanced across the driveway, gave a low cry, and ran away to her room. Pollyanna followed her aunt's glance and saw the carriage pull in front of the house. "Dr. Chilton! Dr. Chilton!" she called out with delight. "Did you want to see me?"

"Yes," the doctor said, a little seriously.

But on her way to greet the doctor, Pollyanna ran into her aunt, angrily untying the lace shawl. "Pollyanna, how could you?" she moaned. "To dress me up this way—and then let someone see me!"

Pollyanna stopped. "But you look lovely, Aunt Polly. Perfectly lovely! And . . ."

"'Lovely'!" said the woman bitterly, throwing off the shawl and attacking her hair with shaking fingers.

"Oh, Aunt Polly! Please, please let the hair stay!"

"Stay? Like this?" Harshly, Miss Polly pulled back her hair so tightly that the last little curl lay dead at her fingertips.

"Oh, dear! And you did look so pretty," Pollyanna almost sobbed as she hurried outside.

The doctor greeted her and explained, "I've 'prescribed' you for a patient. And he's asked me to bring him the 'prescription.' Will you go?"

"You mean, to the drug store?" asked Pollyanna, a little confused.

The doctor smiled. "Not exactly. What I meant was that Mr. John Pendleton would like to see you. And I think that would be good for him. Will you go?"

"I'd love to!" exclaimed Pollyanna. "Let me ask Aunt Polly."

A few moments later, Pollyanna returned, looking serious.

"Doesn't your aunt want you to go?" asked the doctor.

"Yes," sighed Pollyanna. "She wants me to go— but maybe a little too much."

"Too much?"

Pollyanna sighed again. "She said, 'Yes, yes. Run along. Go. I wish you'd gone earlier.'"

After a while, the doctor asked, "Wasn't that your aunt sitting with you in the sunroom?"

"Yes. And that's the problem, I guess. You see,

I'd dressed her up in a perfectly lovely lace shawl I found in the attic. And I'd fixed up her hair and put in a rose. And she looked so pretty. Didn't *you* think she looked just lovely?"

The doctor didn't answer for a moment. Then he said very quietly, "Yes, Pollyanna. I thought she did look just lovely."

"Did you? I'm so glad! I'll tell her," she nodded happily.

"Oh, no, Pollyanna! Never!" he exclaimed.

"Why not, Dr. Chilton? I should think you'd be glad . . ."

"But she might not be," the doctor interrupted.

Pollyanna thought this over. Then she sighed, "Maybe she wouldn't be glad. I remember now. It was when she saw you that she ran. And she talked afterward about being seen all dressed up."

"I thought as much," said the doctor, under his breath.

"I still don't see why she was upset when she looked so pretty."

The doctor said nothing. In fact, he didn't speak again until they had arrived at the big stone house where John Pendleton was lying in bed with a broken leg.

Chapter 17

Just Like a Book

For once, John Pendleton greeted Pollyanna with a smile. "Well, Miss Pollyanna, you must be a very forgiving person to come see me today."

"Why, Mr. Pendleton, I was *glad* to come see you. Why shouldn't I be?"

"Well, you know, I was pretty cranky the day you brought me the ham. And I was really grumpy the day you found me with the broken leg. By the way, I don't think I've ever thanked you for that. You must be a very forgiving to see me after I treated you so ungratefully!"

"But I was glad to find you. Not that I was glad your leg was broken, of course," she corrected quickly.

John Pendleton smiled. "I understand. Your words do sometimes get away from you, don't they, Miss Pollyanna? I do thank you, however.

And I think you're a very brave little girl to do what you did. And I thank you for the ham, too."

"Did you like it?" asked Pollyanna.

"Very much. I don't suppose there's any more today that your Aunt Polly *didn't* send, is there?" he asked with an odd grin.

Pollyanna, worried now, began to blush. "No, sir. And I didn't mean to be rude the other day when I said that Aunt Polly did *not* send the ham."

John Pendleton had stopped smiling. He seemed to be gazing through and beyond Pollyanna. Finally, he sighed and said, "Well, well. This will never do! I didn't ask for you to come here to see me moping again."

John Pendleton asked Pollyanna to bring him a carved wooden box. It was filled with wonderful treasures that he had picked up during his many years of travel. After listening to an entertaining story about a little jade statue from India, Pollyanna murmured, "Well, I guess they were right to take a little boy from India. But I still can't help wishing they'd wanted Jimmy Bean, too."

But John Pendleton did not seem to hear. Once again, his eyes seemed to gaze through Pollyanna to some other place and time.

Soon they were talking about Pollyanna, too—and Nancy, and Aunt Polly, and even her life long ago in a faraway Western town.

When it was time for Pollyanna to go, the usually stern John Pendleton said to her in a warm, tender voice, "Little girl, I'd like you to come see me often. Will you? I'm lonely, and I need you. When I first found out who you were, I thought that I never wanted to see you again. You reminded me of some—of something I've been trying for years to forget. But then I realized that *not* seeing you was making me remember even more of the things I was trying to forget. So now I want you to come. Will you please, little girl?"

"Why, yes, Mr. Pendleton," Pollyanna promised, her eyes glowing with sympathy for the sad-faced man lying in front of her. "I'd love to come!"

"Thank you," said John Pendleton, gently.

That evening, Pollyanna told Nancy all about the wonderful things in Mr. Pendleton's beautiful carved box.

"And to think," sighed Nancy, "that he showed you all those things—the man who's so cranky that he talks to no one—no one!

"Oh, but he isn't cranky, Nancy. Only on the outside. I don't see why everybody thinks he's so bad. They wouldn't if they knew him."

"But what I don't get," continued Nancy, "is why he likes you so much, Miss Pollyanna—not meaning any offense, of course. He's just not the sort of man who usually enjoys kids."

Pollyanna smiled happily. "Well, maybe he just doesn't like seeing them *all* of the time. Why, today he told me that he used to think he never wanted to see me again. That's because I reminded him of something he wanted to forget. But then . . ."

Nancy interrupted. "Did he say what it was you reminded him of?"

"No. He just said it was something."

"The Mystery!" Nancy exclaimed in wonder. "Why, it's just like one of those mystery books I love to read! Only it's happening right here under our noses. Now tell me, Miss Pollyanna. Answer me straight and true. Wasn't it after he found out that you were Miss Polly's niece that he said he never wanted to see you again?"

"Why, yes."

"I thought as much," Nancy declared triumphantly. "And Miss Polly wouldn't send the ham herself, would she?"

"No."

"And you told him she didn't send it?"

"Why, yes. I . . ."

"And that's when he began to act strangely— right after he found out you were her niece?"

"Why, yes," Pollyanna admitted.

"Then I've figured it out!" Nancy glanced over her shoulder to make sure no one was listening. Then she announced, "Mr. John Pendleton was Miss Polly Harrington's boyfriend!"

"But, Nancy! He couldn't be! She doesn't even like him," Pollyanna objected.

"Of course she doesn't! That's the lovers' quarrel!"

Pollyanna still didn't believe her. But then Nancy explained, "It's like this. Mr. Tom told me that Miss Polly once had a boyfriend. I couldn't believe it—not her! But Mr. Tom said her old boyfriend was living right here in this town. And now I know it was John Pendleton! Isn't he mysterious? Doesn't he shut himself up alone in that big house and never speak to anyone? Didn't he act strangely when he found out you were Miss Polly's niece? And didn't he admit that you reminded him of something he wants to forget? And Miss Polly saying she wouldn't send him any ham! Why, Miss Pollyanna, it's as plain as the nose on your face!"

"Oh!" gasped Pollyanna, in wide-eyed amazement. "But Nancy, if they loved each other, wouldn't they have made up by now? Both of them all alone, all these years. I should think they'd be glad to make up!"

"I guess you're not old enough to know much about lovers, Miss Pollyanna. But it sure would be pretty amazing if you could get those two to play the 'glad game.' Then they really might be glad to make up. But I guess there's not much chance of that happening."

Pollyanna didn't say anything. But when she went up to her room, her face was very thoughtful.

Chapter
18

Prisms

For the rest of the summer, Pollyanna often visited the big house on Pendleton Hill. But she didn't feel that her visits were very successful. For John Pendleton never seemed any happier when she was there. At least, that's what Pollyanna thought.

Still, he often invited her to come. And when she was there, he talked to her and showed her interesting and beautiful books, pictures, and souvenirs. He seemed to enjoy listening to Pollyanna talk, which she liked to do. But she was never sure what she said that would suddenly bring that pale, painful look to his face.

Twice she had tried to tell him about the "glad game." But as soon as she mentioned her father, John Pendleton abruptly changed the subject.

Now Pollyanna was sure that John Pendleton was Aunt Polly's old boyfriend. And with all the strength of her loving, loyal heart, she wished she could in some way bring happiness into their miserably lonely lives. But when she talked to Mr. Pendleton about her aunt, he sometimes seemed irritated. And when she tried to talk to her aunt about Mr. Pendleton, Miss Polly always changed the subject. Of course, she did the same thing when Pollyanna talked about other people, like Dr. Chilton. In fact, Aunt Polly seemed especially bitter about Dr. Chilton. Was it because he'd seen her in the sunroom with the rose in her hair and the beautiful lace shawl draped across her shoulders?

Once when Pollyanna had a cold, Aunt Polly said, "If you are not better by tonight, I shall send for the doctor."

"In that case, I'm going to be worse," said Pollyanna with delight. "I'd love to have Dr. Chilton come see me!"

Her aunt looked horrified. "It will not be Dr. Chilton, Pollyanna," she said sternly. "Dr. Chilton is not our family physician. If you are worse, I shall send for Dr. Warren."

Later that evening, Pollyanna explained to her aunt, "I'm glad I got better and you didn't have to call a doctor. Of course, I like Dr. Warren. But I'm afraid Dr. Chilton would be hurt if I didn't have him come. After all, it really wasn't his fault that he happened to see you when I dressed you up so pretty that day."

"That's enough, Pollyanna. I really do not wish to discuss Dr. Chilton—or his feelings."

Later that August, Pollyanna went to visit John Pendleton early one sunny morning. That's when she saw the flaming band of red and blue and orange and gold and green and violet lying across his pillow. She stopped short in amazed delight.

"Why, Mr. Pendleton! It's a baby rainbow that's come inside to pay you a visit! How did it get in?"

"Well," he grumbled wearily, "I suppose it 'got in' through the beveled edge of that glass thermometer in the window. The sunlight strikes it in the morning, even though it's not supposed to hang in the sun."

"But it's so pretty, Mr. Pendleton! If the thermometer was mine, I'd hang it in the sun all day long!"

"But if it hung in the sun all day, you couldn't use the thermometer to tell how hot or cold it was."

"I wouldn't care," said Pollyanna, fascinated by the brilliant band of colors on the pillow. "Why would anybody care about the temperature if they were living in a rainbow?"

The man laughed. Suddenly he had an idea. First he asked the maid to bring him the glass pendants from the candelabra in the dining room. Then he invited Pollyanna to hang them, one by one, on the curtain rod. "If you really want to live in a rainbow, I suppose we'll just have to have a rainbow for you to live in!"

Eagerly she hung all the pendants in the sunlit window. When she had finished, the dreary bedroom had become a fairyland. Everywhere were bits of red and green, violet and orange, gold and blue. The wall, the floor, the chairs, and even the bed were aflame with shimmering bits of color.

"Oh! Oh! Oh! How lovely!" Pollyanna exclaimed, laughing. "Well I guess the sun itself is trying to play the game now," forgetting that she hadn't yet told Mr. Pendleton about the "glad game." "Oh, how I wish I had a lot of those little glass things! How I'd like to give them to Aunt Polly and Mrs. Snow and lots of people! Then they'd be glad, all right! Why, don't you think that if Aunt Polly lived in a rainbow like that, she'd be so glad she just couldn't help banging doors?"

Mr. Pendleton laughed. "Well, from what I know of your aunt, it might take more than a few prisms in the sunlight to make her glad enough to bang doors. But tell me. What's this about a game?"

So this time Pollyanna told him—starting with the crutches that should have been a doll.

When she finished, she sighed, still afraid that she might have said something wrong. "Now you know why I said the sun was trying to play the game."

For a moment there was silence. Then Mr. Pendleton said softly and a little unsteadily, "But I'm thinking that the very finest prism of all is you, Pollyanna."

"Oh, but I don't spread around beautiful reds and greens and purples when the sun shines through me!"

"Don't you?" the man smiled, with tears in his eyes.

"No," Pollyanna said sadly. "The sun doesn't make anything except freckles out of me."

The man laughed again. But strangely, the laugh sounded almost like a sob.

Chapter
19

Which Is Somewhat Surprising

Pollyanna started school in September, and was happy to be with boys and girls her own age. School was, in some ways, a surprise to Pollyanna. And Pollyanna was, in many ways, a surprise to her school. But soon Pollyanna and her school soon learned to enjoy each other. And finally Pollyanna admitted that going to school really was "living," after all.

But school gave Pollyanna less time to spend with her old friends. She did not forget them, though, and gave them as much time as she could. Perhaps John Pendleton missed her the most.

One Saturday afternoon he asked Pollyanna, a little impatiently, "See here, little girl. How would you like to come and live with me? I hardly see you at all these days."

Pollyanna laughed. "I thought you didn't like to have people around."

"But that was before you taught me to play that wonderful game of yours."

"Oh, you say you're glad for things. But you aren't really," Pollyanna argued. "You know you don't play the game the right way, Mr. Pendleton."

The man's face suddenly became very serious. "That's why I want you. Won't you come and help me play it?"

Pollyanna looked upset. "Why, Mr. Pendleton. You know I can't. I'm Aunt Polly's!"

A painful look crossed his face. "You're no more hers than . . ." he answered fiercely, then changed his tone. "Would you come if she let you?"

Pollyanna frowned in deep thought. "But Aunt Polly has been so good to me. She took me when I didn't have anybody left but the Ladies' Aid, and . . ."

Again, that painful look crossed his face. But his time he answered quietly and very sadly, "Pollyanna, many long years ago I loved somebody very much. I'd hoped to bring her, one day, to this house. I pictured how happy we'd be together in our home for many long years to come."

"Yes," Pollyanna nodded, her eyes shining with sympathy.

"But, well, I didn't bring her here. Never mind why. And ever since, this great big place has been just a house—not a home. It takes a loving person's hand and heart—or the presence of a child—to make a home. And I have not had either. So now will you come, my dear?"

Pollyanna sprang to her feet, her face glowing. "You mean, Mr. Pendleton, that you wish you'd had that person's hand and heart all this time?"

"Why, yes, Pollyanna."

"Oh, I'm so glad!" sighed the little girl, relieved. "Now you can take us both. And everything will be lovely."

"Take you both?" the man asked, confused.

"Well, Aunt Polly hasn't agreed yet. But I'm sure she will if you tell her just like you told me. And then we'd both come, of course."

A look of real terror came to the man's eyes. "Aunt Polly? *Here?*"

"Oh, so you'd rather go *there?*" she asked. "Of course, her house isn't quite as pretty, but . . ."

"Pollyanna," the man asked gently, "what *are* you talking about?"

"Where we're going to live, of course. At first I thought you meant here. You said it was here that you'd wanted Aunt Polly's hand and heart all these years to make this a home, and . . ."

The man gasped, unable to speak.

The next moment, the maid announced that Dr. Chilton had arrived.

Pollyanna stood up to leave. But first John Pendleton turned to her anxiously. "Pollyanna, for heaven's sake, don't tell anyone about our talk," he begged her.

"Of course I won't! I know you'd rather tell her yourself!" she called merrily as she skipped out of the room.

John Pendleton slumped limply back in his chair.

A minute later, the doctor was checking his patient's pulse. He was alarmed by the rapid beat. "What's up?" demanded the doctor.

John Pendleton smiled. "Overdose of your medicine, I guess," he chuckled, as he watched Pollyanna skipping down the driveway.

Chapter 20

Which is More Surprising

The next day, when Pollyanna was walking home, Dr. Chilton drove up to her in his carriage. "How about if I take you home, Pollyanna? I was just on my way to tell you that Mr. Pendleton really wants to see you this afternoon. He says it's very important."

Pollyanna nodded happily and climbed into the carriage. "I know what it's about, too!"

The doctor looked surprised.

"And it's so exciting and lovely—just like a story," Pollyanna continued joyfully. Then she burst out, "He said not to tell anyone. But I'm sure he wouldn't mind your knowing. He meant not to tell it to *her*."

"Her?"

"Yes. Aunt Polly. And of course, he'd want to tell her himself. After all, he is her boyfriend."

"Boyfriend!" the doctor exclaimed.

"Oh, yes," nodded Pollyanna happily. "That's what makes it like a story. Of course, I didn't know until Nancy told me. She said that Aunt Polly had a boyfriend many years ago, but they got into a fight. At first, she didn't know who he was. But now I've figured it out. It was Mr. Pendleton, you know!"

"Oh," the doctor said quietly. "No, I didn't know."

"Yes. And I'm so glad now. It's come out lovely. Mr. Pendleton asked me to come and live with him. But of course I wouldn't leave Aunt Polly like that. She's been so good to me. But then he told me about the loving person's hand and heart that he used to want. And now he wants it again. So once he makes up with Aunt Polly, everything will be all right. And Aunt Polly and I will both go to live with him. Or else he'll come to live with us. Of course, Aunt Polly doesn't know yet. And we still have to work out some of the details. So that's why he wants to see me right away."

With a strange little smile, Dr. Chilton said, "Oh, yes. Now I can imagine why Mr. Pendleton is anxious to see you right away."

As they pulled into the driveway, Pollyanna pointed to a window. "There's Aunt Polly now! I'll just run in and ask her if I can see Mr. Pendleton."

But by the time the doctor looked up, he said, "No. She isn't there—not anymore." Suddenly his lips had lost their smile.

John Pendleton was waiting nervously for Pollyanna. As soon as he saw her, he began, "Pollyanna, I've been trying all night to figure out what you meant yesterday—about wanting your Aunt Polly's hand and heart all those years."

"Oh, just that I was glad you were still in love with her after all these years."

"In love? With your Aunt Polly?"

"Why, Mr. Pendleton, Nancy said you were!"

"Indeed!" the man grunted. "Well, I'm afraid that Nancy was wrong."

"Then, you weren't Aunt Polly's boyfriend?" Pollyanna asked, her voice filled with tragic dismay.

"Never!"

"So it isn't all coming out like in a story? Oh, dear! And it was all going so splendidly!" Pollyanna almost sobbed. "I'd have been so glad to come here with Aunt Polly!"

"And now you won't come?" the man asked, without looking at her.

"Of course not! I'm Aunt Polly's."

The man turned to Pollyanna and said almost fiercely, "Before you were hers, Pollyanna, you were your mother's. And it was your mother's hand and heart that I wanted all those long years ago."

"My mother's!"

"Yes. I didn't mean to tell you. But perhaps it's better, after all, that I tell you now." John Pendleton's face had grown very pale. He was having trouble speaking. "I loved your mother. But she didn't love me. After a while, she went away with your father. And the whole world suddenly seemed to turn black. For many years I was a cranky, crabby, unlovable man. But then one day you danced into my life. You were like one of those prisms—sparkling my dreary old world with your own bright cheeriness. And now I want you to stay with me forever. Won't you please, Pollyanna?"

"But Mr. Pendleton. What about Aunt Polly?" Pollyanna answered, her eyes blurred with tears.

"What about *me*? How am I going to be 'glad' about anything without you? Before you came, I wasn't even glad enough to live! But if I had you for my own little girl, I'd be glad for anything. And I'd try to make you glad, too, my dear. I'd give you whatever you wanted. I'd spend all my money—every single cent—just to make you happy."

Pollyanna looked shocked. "Why, Mr. Pendleton! I'd never let you spend the money on me—not the money you've been saving to give to charities!"

The man blushed in embarrassment. He started to speak, but Pollyanna kept talking.

"Besides, with all your money, you don't need me to make you glad for things. You make other people glad by giving them things. So that must make you feel glad yourself! Why, look at those prisms you gave Mrs. Snow, and the coin you gave Nancy on her birthday, and . . ."

By now, John Pendleton was feeling very ashamed. After all, he'd never given much money to charities. "Never mind about all that," he interrupted her. "What I gave was because of you. And that only goes to prove how much I need you, little girl. If I'm ever going to really play the 'glad game,' Pollyanna, you'll have to come and play it with me."

The little girl frowned. "But Aunt Polly's been so good to me," she began.

The man interrupted her, annoyed and impatient. "Of course she's been good to you! But I'm sure she doesn't want you half as much as I do!"

"Why, Mr. Pendleton. I know she's glad to have . . ."

"Glad!" the man interrupted, having completely lost his patience. "I'll bet Miss Polly doesn't know how to be glad for anything! Oh, she does her duty. She always does. I'll admit that we haven't been very friendly for the past fifteen or twenty years. But I know—everyone knows—that she isn't a 'glad' kind of person. She doesn't know how to be glad. So you just ask her if you can come live with me. And you'll see that she'll let you come here!"

Pollyanna sighed and stood up. "All right. I'll ask her. Anyway, I'm glad I didn't tell her about our talk yesterday. Then she might have thought you wanted her, too."

John Pendleton nodded grimly.

"I didn't mention it to anyone," Pollyanna continued. "No one except the doctor, since I knew you wouldn't mind."

"The doctor!" John Pendleton gasped. "Not Dr. Chilton?"

"Yes, of course. You know, when he came to get me."

"Well, of all the . . ." muttered the man, slumping back in his chair. Then he sat up with sudden interest. "And what did Dr. Chilton say?"

Pollyanna frowned. "Not much. He did say, though, that he could imagine why you wanted to see me right away."

"Oh, he did, did he?" John Pendleton said, with a strange little laugh.

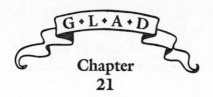

G · L · A · D

Chapter
21

A Question Answered

The sky was darkening fast as Pollyanna hurried home from John Pendleton's house. A thunderstorm seemed to be approaching quickly. Halfway home, Nancy met her with an umbrella. But by then, the storm had shifted away.

"It was Miss Polly that wanted me to come get you," Nancy explained. "She was worried about you!"

Pollyanna didn't answer. She was still thinking about the question she had to ask her aunt.

"I said your aunt was *worried* about you!" Nancy repeated, emphasizing her words.

"Oh," sighed Pollyanna. "I'm sorry. I didn't mean to scare her."

"Well, I'm glad you did!" Nancy answered. "I really am."

Pollyanna stared in shock. "You're *glad* that Aunt Polly was scared about me! Why, Nancy, *that's* not the way to play the game. You shouldn't be glad for things like that!"

Now Nancy looked surprised. "Don't you realize what it means that Miss Polly was worried about you?"

"Why, it means she was worried. And worried is a horrible way to feel."

Nancy shook her head. "In this case, it means that Miss Polly's finally becoming almost human, with human feelings about you. And not just doing her duty."

Pollyanna frowned. "So you think Aunt Polly likes having me here? Do you think she'd mind if I wasn't here any more?"

Until today, Nancy had dreaded this question. How could she answer it honestly without cruelly hurting Pollyanna? But now she felt she could truly reassure this little girl, who had so much love to share. "Well, didn't she send me here with an umbrella just because there was one little cloud in the sky? And didn't she make me carry all your things downstairs just so you could have the pretty room you wanted. And when you think how at first she hated to have . . ." Nancy caught herself just in time. "And it's not just things I can put my fingers on, either. Like how you've been softening her up—with the cat and the dog and the way she speaks to me now. Would she miss you? Why, Miss Pollyanna, there's no telling what she'd do if you weren't there!"

Pollyanna's face lit up with sudden joy. "Oh, Nancy! I'm so glad! Glad! *Glad!* You don't know how glad I am that Aunt Polly actually wants me!"

"I could never leave her now," Pollyanna thought later that evening. "I always knew I wanted to live with Aunt Polly. But I never knew how much I wanted *Aunt Polly* to want to live with *me!*"

Pollyanna dreaded having to tell John Pendleton what she'd decided. She was very fond of him. And she felt very sorry for him, too—maybe because he felt so sorry for himself. Pollyanna felt sad about the long, lonely life that had made him so unhappy. And she felt bad that it was all because of her mother. Soon, once the maid and the nurse left, the big gray house would again be filled with silent rooms, littered floors, a messy desk. Pollyanna's heart ached for his loneliness. She wished that somewhere she could find someone who might—

Suddenly she gave a little shout of joy at the thought that had come to her.

The next day, Pollyanna hurried up the hill to John Pendleton's house.

"Well, Pollyanna? Am I going to play the 'glad game' all the rest of my life?" the man asked gently.

"Oh, yes!" exclaimed Pollyanna. "I've thought of the very gladdest kind of thing for you to do, and . . ."

"But with *you?*" he asked, a little more sternly.

"No, but . . ."

"Oh, Pollyanna! You aren't going to say 'no,' are you?" he interrupted, his voice filled with emotion.

"I've got to, Mr. Pendleton. Truly I do. Aunt Polly . . ."

"Did she *refuse* to let you come?"

"I—I didn't actually ask her," the little girl stammered, upset that her friend looked so hurt.

"Pollyanna! You didn't even ask her!"

"I couldn't, sir. Truly I couldn't. You see, I found out without asking. Now I know that Aunt Polly wants me with her. And I want to stay, too. She's been good to me. I think sometimes she's beginning to be glad for things. And you know she never used to be that way. You said so yourself. Oh, Mr. Pendleton, I couldn't leave Aunt Polly now!"

There was a long silence. At last the man spoke. "I see." Then he added very quietly, "I won't ever ask you again."

"But I haven't told you yet about the gladdest thing you *can* do," she said eagerly.

"Not me, Pollyanna."

"Yes, you, sir. You said it takes a loving person or a child's presence to make a home. Well, I can get one for you. Not me, of course, but another child."

"You're the only one I want!" he said, indignantly.

"But you're so kind and good! Just think of all the prisms and coins and money you've saved for charities and . . ."

"Pollyanna!" he interrupted angrily. "I keep trying to tell you. There is no money for charities. I've never sent them a penny in my entire life!"

Instead of bitter disappointment, Pollyanna's eyes showed only surprise and joy. "Oh, I'm so glad!" she exclaimed, clapping her hands. "That is," she added, blushing, "I feel sad about the charities. But I'm so glad you'd rather have Jimmy Bean."

"Have *who?*"

"Jimmy Bean. He'll be so glad to be your 'child's presence.'"

"Well, *I* won't!" he announced. "Pollyanna, this is sheer nonsense!"

"You mean you won't take him?"

"That's exactly what I mean."

"But he'd be a lovely child's presence," Pollyanna insisted, almost crying. "And you couldn't be lonely with Jimmy around."

"I don't doubt that. But I think I'd prefer being lonely."

Suddenly Pollyanna remembered something Nancy had once told her about John Pendleton. "So you think it's better to have a big old dead skeleton somewhere in your house than a nice live little boy? Well, I think you're wrong!"

"*Skeleton?*"

"Yes. Nancy said you had one in your closet somewhere."

Suddenly the man threw back his head and laughed. "I guess I do have a 'skeleton in the closet.' But it's not the kind you think. What Nancy meant is this. I've gotten used to hiding certain things that happened in the past. But I agree that a 'nice live little boy' would be far better than a sad old secret memory. So why don't you tell me a little more about this nice little boy?"

Was it the sudden laughter that cleared the air? Or the way Pollyanna told Jimmy Bean's sad story that touched a heart that was already strangely softened? Whatever the reason, Mr. John Pendleton invited Pollyanna to bring Jimmy Bean to visit him the very next Saturday afternoon.

"I'm so glad! And I'm sure you'll like him," Pollyanna sighed. "I do so want Jimmy Bean to have a home—and people who care."

Sermons and Woodboxes

On her way home through Pendleton Woods, Pollyanna saw the Reverend Paul Ford, sitting at the foot of a tree.

The minister knew he needed to do something. But what? The people in his parish were constantly quarreling with each other. Some were even leaving the church because of the arguments and hurtful gossip. Reverend Ford had decided that it was time to scold his parishioners for their poor behavior. He'd even found verses from the Bible that would strike fear in their hearts. Sitting alone in the woods, the minister made a few notes about next Sunday's sermon. But when he tried saying it out loud, he realized that his words sounded bitter and mean. With a moan, he crumpled his notes and covered his face with his hands.

When Pollyanna saw the minister, she gasped, "Oh, Mr. Ford! You haven't broken your leg or anything, have you?"

"No, dear. I'm just resting here. And I haven't broken anything—at least, nothing that doctors can fix."

Pollyanna's eyes glowed with tender sympathy. "I know what you mean. Something's bothering you. Father used to feel like that, lots of times. I guess most ministers do. After all, so much depends on them."

The minister stared at the ground, saying nothing.

Pollyanna, feeling sorry for him, tried to cheer him up. "It's a nice day, isn't it?"

"What? Oh, yes."

"Don't you love being out here in the woods?"

This time there was no reply. So Pollyanna tried a different method. "Do you like being a minister?"

"Do I like—? Why, what a strange question! Why do you ask, my dear?"

"Oh, it's just the way you look. My father used to look like that sometimes."

"Did he?"

"Yes. And I used to ask him if he was glad he was a minister."

The man smiled a little sadly. "Well, what did he say?"

"Oh, he always said he was. But he also said he couldn't have done it without the rejoicing verses."

"The what?" he asked in wonder.

"The rejoicing verses. At least, that's what Father called them," Pollyanna laughed merrily. "You know. The verses in the Bible that start with 'Be glad' or 'Rejoice greatly' or 'Shout for joy.' There are so many of them! Why, once when Father felt really bad, he counted them. There were 800 of them!"

"Oh," the minister murmured, thinking of the sermon he'd started to write. "And your father liked those 'rejoicing verses'?"

"Oh, yes," Pollyanna nodded. "He felt better as soon as he thought to count them. He said that God took the trouble to tell us 800 times to be glad and rejoice. So maybe we really ought to do it. And that's what made him think of the game."

"And what game might that be?" asked the minister.

"About finding something in everything to be glad for." And once more Pollyanna told her story about the crutches.

That evening, the minister sat thinking about his sermon. He pictured a little Western town with a minister who was poor, sick, worried, and almost alone in the world—counting how many times the Bible said to "rejoice" and "be glad."

Then he noticed an article in a magazine his wife had left lying open on his desk. It told the story of a boy who had refused to put wood into his mother's wood box. His father then said to him, "Tom, I'm sure you'll be glad to go and bring in some wood for your mother." And without a word, Tom went. Why? Just because his father showed that he expected Tom to do the right thing. What if he'd said instead, "Tom, I heard what you said to your mother, and I'm ashamed of you"?

The article then explained, "What people need is encouragement. Instead of telling people about their faults, tell them what makes them good. Try to pull them out of their bad habits. Show them their better selves—their real selves. When you look for the bad and expect to find it, that's what you'll get. When you know you'll find the good, that's what you'll get. What's in people's hearts and minds—good or bad—spreads from one person to another. That's why all it takes is one helpful, hopeful person to change an entire town."

The next Sunday, the Reverend Paul Ford gave a sermon that inspired every man, woman, and child in his congregation. But he never scolded anyone. Instead, he encouraged them to rejoice and be glad in all their good thoughts and all their kind deeds.

Chapter
23

An Accident

One day, Mrs. Snow asked Pollyanna to go to Dr. Chilton's office to pick up a prescription.

When she arrived, Pollyanna asked the doctor, "This is your home, isn't it?"

The doctor smiled a little sadly. "Yes—if you could call it that. But they're just rooms, Pollyanna, not a home."

Pollyanna nodded sympathetically. "I know. Mr. Pendleton told me it takes a loving person's hand and heart—or the presence of a child—to make a home. Why don't you get some loving person's hand and heart, Dr. Chilton? Or you could take Jimmy Bean if Mr. Pendleton doesn't want him."

"So that's what Mr. Pendleton says, does he?"

"Yes. He says his is just a house, too. So why

don't you, Dr. Chilton?"

"Why don't I what?"

"Get a loving person's hand and heart. And speaking of that, I need to tell you I made a mistake. It wasn't Aunt Polly that Mr. Pendleton loved long ago. I hope you didn't tell anyone," she said, anxiously.

"No, I didn't tell anyone," the doctor answered, a little strangely.

Pollyanna sighed in relief. "When I told Mr. Pendleton you were the only person I told, I thought he looked sort of funny."

"He did, did he?" the doctor said, trying not to laugh.

"Yes. But why don't you get a loving person's hand and heart?"

After a moment, the doctor answered sadly, "Sometimes they're hard to get."

"But I should think *you'd* be able to get them."

"Thank you," the doctor laughed.

Pollyanna frowned. "Dr. Chilton, did you, too, once try to get somebody's hand and heart—and couldn't?"

"Never mind about that now, Pollyanna," he said, handing her the prescription. And don't worry too much about other people's troubles."

"Thank you, sir," Pollyanna murmured. And then she added, her face brightening, "Anyway, I'm glad it wasn't my mother's hand and heart you wanted and couldn't get. Goodbye, Dr. Chilton!"

Then the accident happened. It was on the last day of October, and Pollyanna was hurrying home from school. She saw a car approaching her. But she thought she had enough time to cross the road safely.

No one really knew what happened or who was to blame. But at 5 o'clock, Pollyanna was carried, limp and unconscious, into the little room that was so dear to her. A very pale Aunt Polly and a weeping Nancy tenderly put her to bed.

After Dr. Warren arrived, Nancy went to talk to Old Tom in the garden. "If you'd seen her aunt's face and shaking hands, you'd know it wasn't just 'duty' that was eating away at her."

"Is she hurt bad?" the old man asked, his voice shaking.

"There's no telling," sobbed Nancy. "She was so pale and still I thought she was dead. But Miss Polly said she could feel her heart beating and hear her breathing."

"So where is she hurt?"

"I don't know," moaned Nancy. "Miss Polly seemed worried about infernal injuries."

"I guess you mean *internal* injuries, Nancy—injuries inside her body. I think the whole darn thing is 'infernal.' But I don't think Miss Polly would use a word like that."

After examining Pollyanna, Dr. Warren looked very serious. He shook his head slowly, and said that only time would tell. Pollyanna still wasn't fully conscious. But she seemed to be resting as comfortably as possible. A nurse would come and stay with her. That was all. Nancy, still sobbing, went back to the kitchen. Miss Polly stayed in Pollyanna's room, looking even paler and more worried than before.

The next morning Pollyanna finally opened her eyes and realized where she was. "What's the matter, Aunt Polly? Isn't it daytime? Why aren't I up yet?" she asked anxiously. Then she tried to lift herself. "Why, Aunt Polly! I can't get up," she moaned, falling back on the pillow.

"Don't try just yet, dear," her aunt soothed very quietly.

"But what's the matter? Why can't I get up?"

Miss Polly tried to swallow the lump in her throat. "You were hurt, dear, by a car. But never mind that now. Just try to rest."

"Hurt? Oh, yes. I was running." Pollyanna's eyes were dazed. She touched her forehead. "Why, there are bandages on it, and it hurts!"

"Yes, dear. But never mind. Just rest."

"But Aunt Polly, I feel so funny—and so bad! My legs feel so strange. They don't really feel at all!"

Miss Polly couldn't speak. So the nurse who had been standing behind her stepped forward.

"Suppose you let me talk to you now," she began cheerily. "I'm Miss Hunt. I've come to help your aunt take care of you. Right now I'm going to ask you to swallow these little white pills for me."

Pollyanna's eyes grew wild. "But I don't want to be taken care of! I want to get up and go to school. Can't I go to school tomorrow?"

Aunt Polly tried to choke back a cry.

"Tomorrow?" the nurse answered brightly. "Well, I may not let you go out quite that soon, Miss Pollyanna. But just swallow these little pills for me, please. And we'll see what they'll do."

"All right," Pollyanna agreed, somewhat doubtfully. "But I must go to school the day after tomorrow. There are tests that day."

For a few minutes Pollyanna talked about school and the car and how her head ached. But soon her voice trailed into silence, thanks to those little white pills.

Chapter
24

John Pendleton

Pollyanna did not go to school "tomorrow" or "the day after tomorrow." At first she didn't realize how much time had passed. In fact, she wasn't able to think clearly until a week later, when her mind became fully conscious. Then she had to be told all over again what had happened.

"So I'm hurt, but not sick," Pollyanna sighed at last. "Well, I'm glad of that."

"Glad, Pollyanna?" asked her aunt, who was sitting beside the bed.

"Yes. I'd much rather have broken legs like Mr. Pendleton than a lifelong illness like Mrs. Snow. Broken legs get well, and lifelong illnesses don't."

Miss Polly's face grew even paler. She hadn't said anything about broken legs. And she didn't know what to say now.

"I'm glad it isn't smallpox, either. That would be worse than freckles," Pollyanna murmured. She gazed happily at the dancing band of colors that one of the prisms in her window cast onto the ceiling. "And I'm glad it isn't earaches. I've had them, and they're awful. And I'm glad it isn't appendicitis or measles. Because measles are catching, and they wouldn't let you stay here."

"You seem to be glad for a lot of things, my dear," Aunt Polly choked, once again trying to clear the lump in her throat.

Pollyanna laughed softly. "I am. I've been thinking them up—lots of them—while I've been looking up at that rainbow. I love rainbows. And I'm so glad Mr. Pendleton gave me those prisms! I'm even glad for some things I haven't said yet. Why, I'm almost glad that I was hurt."

"Pollyanna!"

Pollyanna laughed softly again. She looked at her aunt, her eyes glowing. "Well, you see, ever since I was hurt, you've called me 'dear' lots of times. And you never did before. I love being called 'dear'—especially by people who are family. Oh, Aunt Polly, I'm so glad you're my family!"

Aunt Polly did not answer. The lump was still in her throat, and her eyes were full of tears.

That afternoon Nancy ran out to tell Old Tom the news. "Mr. Tom! Mr. Tom! You'll never guess what's happened—not in a thousand years!"

"Well, since I'm not going to live that long, I guess you'd better tell me."

"So who do you think is in the living room now with Miss Polly?"

Old Tom shook his head. "Who?"

"Why, it's John Pendleton!"

"You've got to be kidding!"

"Not a bit. There he is, crutches and all! That cranky old man who never talks to anyone—coming to visit Miss Polly!"

"Well, why not?"

"Don't pretend not to know! You were the one who told me Miss Polly'd once had a boyfriend. So I put two and two together and figured Miss Polly and Mr. Pendleton had been in love with each other."

"Mr. Pendleton!" Tom exclaimed, straightening up from his gardening.

"Oh, I know now that he was in love with that dear child's mother, not with Miss Polly. But then I found out that she's been hating him for years—all because of that silly gossip."

"Yes, I remember," nodded Old Tom. "It was a few years after Miss Jennie went off with that minister fellow. Miss Polly tried to be nice to Mr. Pendleton. She felt sorry for him. And maybe she overdid it a little. But then somebody tried to make trouble by starting a rumor about them. About the same time, she started having troubles with her own boyfriend. And that's when she shut up like a clam and wouldn't have anything to do with anybody. Her heart just seemed to turn bitter at the core."

In the Harrington living room, Mr. Pendleton politely tried to stand as Miss Polly stepped swiftly into the room. She told him to stay seated. But she did not offer to shake his hand.

"I came to ask about Pollyanna," he began, a little stiffly.

"Thank you. She is about the same," said Miss Polly coldly.

"The same as—? Won't you tell me *how* she is?" he asked, his voice unsteady.

A quick spasm of pain crossed the woman's face. "I wish I could!"

"You mean, you don't know?"

The woman nodded.

"But the doctor—?"

"Dr. Warren himself doesn't seem to know. He's arranged a consultation with a specialist in New York."

"But what injuries do you know about?"

"A small cut on the head, a few bruises, and an injury to the spine, which . . ." Miss Polly's voice broke. "Which seems to have caused paralysis from the hips down."

The man moaned softly. Then he asked, his voice shaking, "And Pollyanna? How is she taking it?"

"She doesn't understand how bad things really are. And I can't tell her."

"But she must know something!"

Miss Polly struggled to speak through the lump in her throat. "Oh, yes. She knows she can't move. But she thinks her legs are broken. She says she's glad she has broken legs like yours rather than a lifelong illness like Mrs. Snow's. She says that broken legs get well, and the other doesn't. She talks like that all the time until I feel as if—as if . . ."

Through the tears in his own eyes, the man saw that the woman's face was twisted with pain. He remembered how Pollyanna had said, "Oh, I couldn't leave Aunt Polly now!"

As soon as he could control his voice, John Pendleton said very gently, "I suppose you don't know, Miss Harrington, how hard I tried to get Pollyanna to come live with me."

"Pollyanna? With you!"

The man winced, and then said, "Yes. I wanted to adopt her legally—and make her my heir, of course."

The woman wondered if Pollyanna had been tempted by this man's money and social status.

"I am very fond of Pollyanna," the man continued, "both for her sake and for her mother's. I was ready to give Pollyanna all the love I'd been keeping inside for 25 years."

"Love," Miss Polly murmured. Suddenly she remembered why she'd taken this child. And she remembered Pollyanna's saying that very morning how much she loved being called "dear" by people who are family. Surely this lonely little girl would be tempted by love! With a sinking heart, Miss Polly realized how dreary her life would be without Pollyanna.

"And so—?" she asked, afraid of the answer.

The man smiled sadly. "She would not come."

"Why?"

"She would not leave you. She said you had been so good to her. She wanted to stay with you. And she said she thought you wanted her to stay."

Without looking at Miss Polly, John Pendleton started walking toward the door.

But Miss Polly stopped him. She took his hand and said in a trembling voice, "I will let you know as soon as I find out anything definite about Pollyanna. Goodbye. And thank you for coming. Pollyanna will be pleased."

Chapter
25

A Waiting Game

The next day, Miss Polly started preparing Pollyanna for the specialist's visit.

"Pollyanna, my dear," she began gently. "We've decided to have you see another doctor besides Dr. Warren."

Pollyanna's eyes lit up with joy. "Dr. Chilton! Oh, Aunt Polly, I'd so love to have Dr. Chilton! I've wanted him all along. But I was afraid you didn't—you know, because he saw you in the sunroom that day. Oh, I'm so glad you want him, too!"

Aunt Polly looked shocked, then embarrassed, then very upset. But she tried to answer cheerfully, "Oh, no, dear! I wasn't talking about Dr. Chilton at all. This is a new doctor—a very famous doctor from New York. And he knows all about hurts like yours."

Pollyanna's face fell in disappointment. "I doubt he knows half as much as Dr. Chilton."

"Oh, but I'm sure he does, dear."

"But it was Dr. Chilton who fixed Mr. Pendleton's broken leg. So if you don't mind too much, I would like to have Dr. Chilton. Truly I would!"

More upset than ever, Miss Polly said gently, but firmly, "But I do mind, Pollyanna. I mind very much. And for reasons I don't care to discuss right now, I do not wish to involve Dr. Chilton."

"But Aunt Polly! If you loved Dr. Chilton . . ."

"*What*, Pollyanna?" Aunt Polly asked sharply, her cheeks flushing.

"If you loved Dr. Chilton more than the other doctor," Pollyanna sighed, "it might make a difference in how much good he could do. And I love Dr. Chilton."

The next day, Pollyanna again begged her aunt to let her see Dr. Chilton.

And again, Aunt Polly said, "No, dear." But Miss Polly then added that she would do anything—anything but that—to please her dear Pollyanna.

They waited day after day for the specialist to arrive. And Aunt Polly did in fact try to do everything she could to please Pollyanna. Everything, that is, except "that."

One morning, Nancy said to Old Tom, "I'd never have believed it. Miss Polly just hangs around every minute of the day, waiting to do something for that dear child. Why, she even lets Fluffy and Buffy tumble all over the bed just because it pleases Miss Pollyanna! And when Miss Polly's not doing anything else, she moves those little glass pendants around to different windows so the sun will make the 'little rainbows dance.' Why the other day, she even let the nurse do up her hair, with Miss Pollyanna giving instructions from the bed. And ever since Miss Polly's worn her hair like that—just to please that dear child!"

Old Tom chuckled. "Well, it seems like all those curls and ribbons and lace haven't made Miss Polly look any worse!"

"Of course not! Why, she's actually starting to look . . ."

"I told you so," the man nodded. "I told you she wasn't old."

Nancy laughed. "So tell me, Mr. Tom. Just who *was* her boyfriend? You see, there aren't many people I can ask."

Old Tom grinned. "Well, here's one person that isn't answering." Then his eyes darkened. "So how is she today, the little gal?"

Nancy shook her head, her face serious. "She's no different, Mr. Tom. She just lies there and tries to smile and be 'glad' that the sun sets or the moon rises, or some other thing like that. Why, it's enough to make your heart break!"

"I know. It's the 'game,'" Old Tom nodded, blinking back the tears. "She told me all about the game one day when I was grumbling because my back was so crooked."

"What in the world could she find to be glad for that?"

"Well, she said I could be glad I was already partly bent over. That way I didn't have to stoop over so far to do my weeding!"

Nancy laughed a little sadly. "We've been playing the game since she got here. She said she didn't have anyone else to play it with—not even her aunt."

"You mean the little gal hasn't told her yet? Why, she's told everyone else in town! Everybody's been talking about it, ever since she was hurt."

"Well, she didn't tell Miss Polly," Nancy explained. "It was her father's game, and Miss Polly didn't want her to talk about her father."

The old man nodded slowly. "Yes, they were all very bitter about that minister fellow. That's because he took Miss Jennie away from them. And Miss Polly was so fond of her older sister that she never could forgive him."

Waiting for the specialist to arrive was difficult for everyone. The nurse and the doctor were nervous and impatient. Miss Polly was becoming thin and pale. Pollyanna patted the dog, smoothed the cat's fur, and watched the "rainbows" in her room. She sent answers to the many messages of love that were brought to her bedside. But she, too, grew pale and thin.

As for the game, Pollyanna told Nancy how glad she'd be when she could go to school again, and see Mrs. Snow, and visit Mr. Pendleton, and ride with Dr. Chilton. The little girl didn't seem to realize that all this "gladness" was not going to happen soon—if at all. But Nancy did. And she often cried about it when she was alone.

Chapter 26

Through an Open Door

$\mathcal{A}$ week later, Dr. Mead, the specialist, arrived. He was a tall man with kind gray eyes and a cheerful smile. Pollyanna liked him right away and told him so. "You see," Pollyanna explained eagerly, "you look a lot like *my* doctor. Not Dr. Warren, of course. He's Aunt Polly's doctor. My doctor is Dr. Chilton."

"Oh?" asked Dr. Mead, as Miss Polly turned away in embarrassment.

"Yes. You see, I wanted Dr. Chilton all the time. But Aunt Polly wanted you. She said you knew how to fix broken legs like mine. Do you?"

"Only time will tell, little girl," he said gently.

The two doctors examined Pollyanna carefully. Then they stepped into the hallway to speak privately with Miss Polly and the nurse.

Afterward, everyone said that it was the cat's fault. If Fluffy hadn't gone into the bedroom, Pollyanna would not have heard her aunt's words.

But Fluffy did not want to be in the hallway while Pollyanna was in her room. So she pushed open the door and jumped onto the bed. That was when Pollyanna heard Aunt Polly exclaim, "Not that, Doctor! No, not that! You can't mean the child will never walk again!"

Pollyanna cried out in terror, "Aunt Polly! Aunt Polly!"

Then Miss Polly, realizing that Pollyanna had heard her through the open door, gave a moan and fainted.

While the doctors tried to revive Miss Polly, the nurse rushed into the bedroom.

"Miss Hunt, please!" begged Pollyanna. "I want Aunt Polly! I want her right away, please!"

"She can't come in right this minute, dear. What is it?"

"I want to know what she said just now. I want Aunt Polly to tell me it's not true! It's not true!"

The nurse tried to speak, but no words came.

"Miss Hunt! You *heard* her! It *is* true! You mean I can't ever walk again?"

"There, there, dear. Maybe the doctor didn't know. Maybe he was wrong. Lots of things could happen, you know."

"But Aunt Polly said he knows all about—about broken legs like mine!"

"Yes, yes, dear. But doctors sometimes make mistakes. Try not to think about it right now. Please don't, dear."

"But I can't help thinking about it!" Pollyanna cried. "It's all there is now to think about. If I can't walk, how am I going to go school? Or see Mr. Pendleton or Mrs. Snow or—anybody?"

Pollyanna sobbed wildly for a few moments. Then suddenly she stopped crying and looked up, a new terror in her eyes. "Why, Miss Hunt, if I can't walk, how am I ever going to glad for *anything*?"

"There, there, dear. Just take this," the nurse answered, giving Pollyanna some medicine to make her sleep. "Lots of times things aren't half as bad as they seem."

"That sounds like something Father used to say," Pollyanna choked, blinking back the tears. "He said there was something about everything that might be worse. But what could possibly be worse about never walking again?"

Chapter
27

Two Visits

That afternoon, Miss Polly sent Nancy to Mr. John Pendleton's house.

"I'm Nancy, sir," she said respectfully. "Miss Harrington sent me to tell you about Miss Pollyanna."

"Well?" the man asked anxiously.

"She's not 'well' at all, Mr. Pendleton," Nancy choked.

"You don't mean . . ."

"Yes, sir. Dr. Mead said she won't walk again—ever."

For a moment there was absolute silence. Then the man spoke in a quiet, unsteady voice. "Poor little girl! Never to dance in the sunshine again! My little prism girl!"

There was another silence. Then the man asked abruptly, "Of course, she doesn't know yet, does she?"

"But she does, sir!" Nancy sobbed. "The cat pushed open the door, and Miss Pollyanna overheard them talking."

"Poor little girl," he sighed again.

"Yes, sir. It's all so fresh and new to her. And she keeps thinking of new things she won't be able to do now. She's worried, too, because she can't seem to play the 'glad game' anymore. She says she can't think of a thing—not one thing—to be glad for about not walking again."

"Well, why should she?" the man snapped back.

"That's how I felt, too. But then I thought maybe it *would* be easier if she could find something. So I reminded her how she taught other people how to play it—what she told them to do. But she just cries and says it's not the same, somehow. She says it's easy to tell someone with a lifelong illness how to be glad. But it's different when you have the lifelong illness yourself. She says she keeps *telling* herself how glad she is that other people don't have her illness. But all she keeps *thinking* about is how she'll never walk again."

The man did not speak. He sat with his hand over his eyes.

"Then I tried to remind her about what she used to say," Nancy continued quietly. "You know, how the game is even more fun when it's hard. But she says that, too, is different when it really *is* hard."

Nancy started to leave, and then asked timidly, "I don't suppose I could tell Miss Pollyanna that you'd seen Jimmy Bean again, could I?"

"I don't see how, since I haven't seen him. Why?"

"Nothing, sir. It's just that, well, she's feeling bad because now she can't take him to see you again. She's afraid that he didn't look too good the first time. She wants you to see he really could be a lovely 'child's presence' for you. But now, sir, she can't."

It did not take long for the entire town of Beldingsville to learn that the great doctor from New York had said Pollyanna Whittier would never walk again. By now, everybody knew the little freckled-faced girl who always greeted everyone with a smile. And almost everybody knew about Pollyanna's "game." To think that they would never again see that smiling face running down their streets! Or hear that cheerful voice point out the gladness of some everyday experience! It seemed unbelievable, impossible, cruel!

Then they learned what was distressing Pollyanna most of all. Face to face with what had happened to her, Pollyanna could not play the game. She could no longer be glad about *anything*.

That's when the same thought occurred to

all of Pollyanna's friends. Suddenly, to her great surprise, Miss Polly Harrington began to hear from them—men, women, and children. Some people she knew, and some she did not. Some she never suspected that Pollyanna even knew.

Some people came in and sat down stiffly for five or ten minutes. Some stood awkwardly on the porch steps, fumbling with hats or handbags. Some brought books, flowers, or candy. Some cried openly. Some turned their backs to wipe away their tears. But all asked very anxiously about the injured little girl. And all sent her messages.

It was these messages, finally, that stirred Miss Polly to action.

First came Mr. John Pendleton. This time he came without his crutches. "I don't need to tell you how shocked I am," he began, choking back tears. "But is it true that nothing can be done?"

"We're doing everything that Dr. Mead suggested. But he held out almost no hope," Miss Polly said sadly.

John Pendleton's face paled. Then he said, "I have a message for Pollyanna. Will you tell her, please, that I am going to adopt Jimmy Bean. Tell her I thought she would be *glad* to know."

"You're adopting Jimmy Bean!" Miss Polly gasped.

"Yes," he answered proudly. "I think Pollyanna will understand. Please don't forget to tell her I thought she would be—*glad!*"

Miss Polly could hardly believe her ears. John Pendleton—wealthy, independent, gloomy, self-centered—adopt a little boy? And a little boy like Jimmy Bean?

Still in a daze, Miss Polly went upstairs to Pollyanna's room. "Pollyanna, I have a message for you from Mr. John Pendleton. He said he's going to adopt Jimmy Bean. He said he thought you'd be glad to know it."

Pollyanna's sad little face suddenly flamed with joy. "Glad? *Glad*? Why, I guess I *am* glad! Oh, Aunt Polly, I've wanted so much to find a place for Jimmy. And that's such a lovely place! Besides, I'm really glad for Mr. Pendleton, too. You see, now he'll have a child's presence."

"A what?"

"A child's presence. You see, Mr. Pendleton once told me that only a loving person's hand and heart, or a child's presence, could make a home. And now he's got it—a child's presence."

"Oh, I see," said Miss Polly very gently, her eyes stinging with sudden tears.

"Dr. Chilton says so, too—that it takes a loving person's hand and heart, or a child's presence, to make a home," Pollyanna added.

Startled, Miss Polly exclaimed, "Dr. Chilton! He told you that?"

"Yes. And that's why he said he lives in just rooms, and not a home."

Miss Polly did not answer. She was gazing out the window.

"So I asked him why he didn't get a loving person's hand and heart—and have a home."

"Pollyanna!" Miss Polly said sharply, blushing deeply.

"But he looked so sad."

"Well, what did he say?" Miss Polly asked, unable to hold back the question.

"He didn't say anything for a minute. Then he said very quietly that sometimes they're hard to get."

Miss Polly, still blushing, turned again to stare out the window.

Pollyanna sighed. "But I know he wants one. And I wish he could have one, too."

"Why, Pollyanna! How do you know that?"

"Because another time I heard him say something else. He said it very quietly, but I heard him anyway. He said he'd give all the world if only he could have one loving person's hand and heart."

Miss Polly stood up quickly and hurried over to the window.

"Why, Aunt Polly! What's the matter?" Pollyanna asked.

"Nothing, dear. I was just changing the position of this prism," she answered, her whole face now aflame.

Chapter 28

The Game and Its Players

A few days later, Milly Snow came to visit Miss Polly Harrington. "I came to ask about the little girl," she said awkwardly.

"You are very kind to ask. She is about the same. And how is your mother?" Miss Polly asked wearily.

"That's why I came. We think it's so perfectly awful that Pollyanna can't ever walk again. And after all she's done for us! You know, teaching mother how to play the game. Then we heard that she can't play it herself, poor little dear! So we thought if she could only know how much she's done for us, it might help her be glad—at least a little glad . . ."

Miss Polly listened politely, with a puzzled look in her eyes. "I don't think I quite understand, Milly. Just what would you like me to tell my niece?"

"Make her see what she's done for us. Tell her how different Mother is—and me, too. I've been trying to play the game a little myself."

Miss Polly frowned. She wanted to ask what Milly meant by "the game." But Milly rushed on nervously.

"Before Pollyanna, nothing was ever right for mother. She always wanted things to be different. Not that anyone could blame her under the circumstances. But now she lets me keep the shades up. She takes an interest in things. She's actually started knitting baby blankets for hospitals. And she's so *glad* she can do it. And that was all because of Miss Pollyanna. You see, Pollyanna told Mother she could be glad about at least being able to use her hands and arms. So Mother started thinking about something she *could* do with her hands and arms. And now the room's so different—with pink and blue and yellow yarn, and the prisms in the window! So would you please tell Miss Pollyanna that we understand it's all because of her? Maybe if she knows how glad we are that we know her, she might be a little glad that she knows us, too. And . . . and . . ." sighed Milly, as she stood up to leave. "You'll tell her?"

"Of course," Miss Polly murmured, more puzzled than ever.

John Pendleton and Milly Snow were only the first of many visitors. And all had messages—

messages that left Miss Polly more puzzled than ever.

One day Widow Benton came. Miss Polly heard that she was the saddest woman in town, and that she always dressed all in black. But today Mrs. Benton was wearing a pale blue scarf. With tears in her eyes, she asked if she might see Pollyanna.

Miss Polly shook her head. "I'm sorry. But she's not able to see anyone yet."

Mrs. Benton wiped her eyes and turned to go. But suddenly she said, "Miss Harrington, perhaps you'd give her a message? Will you tell her, please, that I've put this on?" she asked, touching the scarf. "The little girl has been trying for so long to get me to wear color. She said my little Freddy would be so glad to see it. You know, he's all I have, now that . . . . So I thought Pollyanna would be glad to know I've begun. If you'd just tell her, *she'll* understand."

Later that morning, another lady came to call. She was dressed in black, and introduced herself as "Mrs. Tarbell."

"I've been staying at the hotel all summer," she explained to Miss Polly. "I've had to take long walks for my health. On one of those walks I met your niece. She's such a dear little girl! I wish I could make you understand what she's been to me. I was very sad when I came up here. Her bright face and cheery ways reminded me of my own little girl—the one I lost years ago. I was so shocked to hear that the poor child had an accident and would never walk again. But when I learned that the dear child was unhappy because she couldn't be glad any longer—well, I just had to come. I want you to give her a message from me. Will you?"

"Certainly," Miss Polly murmured.

"Just tell her, please, that Mrs. Tarbell is glad now. I know it sounds strange, and you don't understand. But if you'll forgive me, I'd rather not explain." The lady's face grew sad. "Your niece will know just what I mean."

Totally mystified now, Miss Polly hurried upstairs to Pollyanna's room. "Pollyanna, do you know a Mrs. Tarbell?"

"Oh, yes. I love Mrs. Tarbell. She's sick, and awfully sad. And she takes long walks. We go together. I mean—we used to." Pollyanna's voice broke, and tears started to roll down her cheeks.

"Well, she's just been here, dear," Miss Polly hurried on. "She left a message for you. But she wouldn't tell me what it meant. She said to tell you that Mrs. Tarbell is glad now."

Pollyanna clapped her hands softly. "Did she say that? Really? Oh, I'm so glad!"

"But, Pollyanna, what did she mean?"

"Why, it's the game, and . . ." Pollyanna stopped short.

"What game?"

"Nothing much, Aunt Polly. That is, I can't talk about it unless I talk about things I'm not supposed to talk about."

That afternoon came the most surprising visit of all. The young woman was wearing high heels, cheap jewelry, and too much makeup. Miss Polly knew her by her reputation, and she was angry that she dared come to her house. Miss Polly did not offer to shake her hand.

The woman asked if she might, for a moment, see Pollyanna. Her eyes were very red, as if she had been crying.

Miss Polly said no.

The woman hesitated, but finally spoke. "My name is Mrs. Payson. I guess you've heard about me, though some things you've heard aren't true. Maybe you don't know that your niece has been visiting our house. She played with my kids and talked to me. She seemed to like it, and to like us. She didn't know that her kind of folks don't generally call on my kind. But maybe if they did call more, Miss Harrington, there wouldn't be so many of my kind. Anyway, she'd come and sit on our doorstep and play with the kids and laugh and—and just be glad. She was always being glad about something. And then, one day, she told us about the game, and tried to get us to play it. Anyway, she didn't do herself any harm. And she did do us some good—a lot of good. She'll never know how much, I hope. Because if she did, she'd know other things about us—things that I don't want her to know.

"Anyway, it's been hard for us this year. My man and me—we were discouraged and ready to get a divorce. And the kids—well, we didn't know what we'd do with the kids. But then came the accident. And we heard how she'll never walk again. And I wish I could give her my own two healthy, but useless legs. She'd do more good running around in them in one hour that I could in a hundred years. But I've noticed that legs aren't always given to those who can use them best. Anyway, we heard that she's worrying her poor little life away because she can't play the game anymore. That there's nothing to be glad about. So I came to tell her that maybe she can be a little glad for us, because we've decided to stick together and play the game ourselves. I know she'll be glad, because she used to feel kind of bad about things we said sometimes. Anyway, we're going to try—because she wanted us to. Will you tell her that, please?"

"Yes, I will," Miss Polly promised. Then suddenly she reached for the other woman's hand. "Thank you for coming, Mrs. Payson."

As soon as she left, Miss Polly hurried into the kitchen. "Nancy!" she demanded sharply. "Nancy, *will* you tell me about this foolish 'game' that the whole town is babbling about? And what, please, does my niece have to do with it? Why is everybody—from Milly Snow to Mrs. Payson—sending her messages that they're 'playing it'? It seems as if everyone in town is wearing blue scarves or stopping family fights or learning to like something they never liked before. And all because of Pollyanna. Now *will* you tell me what this all means?"

Suddenly Nancy burst into tears. "It means that ever since she came here, that dear child has been making the whole town glad. And now they're turning around and trying to make her a little glad, too."

"Glad of what?"

"Just glad! That's the game."

Miss Polly was so frustrated that she actually stamped her foot. "There you go, Nancy. Just like all the rest. *What* game?"

Nancy looked Miss Polly directly in the eye. "I'll tell you, ma'am. It's a game that Miss Pollyanna's father taught her to play. Once she got a pair of crutches in a missionary barrel, when what she wanted was a doll. She started crying, of course. So her father told her that there was something about everything that you could be glad for. And that she could be glad for those crutches."

"Glad for *crutches!*" Miss Polly choked back a sob, thinking about the helpless little legs on the bed upstairs.

"Yes'm. But he told her she could be glad because she didn't need them!"

"Oh!" cried Miss Polly.

"And after that he made a game of finding something in everything to be glad about. They called it the 'just being glad' game. And she's played it ever since."

"But, how—how—?"

"Oh, you'd be surprised how great it works, ma'am. Why she's made me glad, too, about so many things—little things and big things. It makes them so much easier. For instance, I don't mind being named 'Nancy' since she told me I could be glad my name wasn't 'Haphzibah.' And she's actually made me glad for Monday mornings."

"Glad for Monday mornings?"

Nancy laughed. "I know it sounds crazy, ma'am. But she found out that I hated Monday mornings. So she told me I could be gladder about Mondays than any other day of the week— because then it would be a whole week until I had another one! And sure enough, I've thought of it every Monday morning since then. And it has helped, ma'am. Anyway, every time I think of it, it makes me laugh. And laughing helps, you know!"

"But why hasn't she told *me* the game?"

Nancy hesitated. "Begging your pardon, ma'am, but you told her not to talk about her father. So she couldn't tell you. You see, it was her father's game."

Miss Polly bit her lip.

"She wanted to tell you first," Nancy continued. "She taught it to me so she could have someone to play it with."

"And the others?" asked Miss Polly, her voice shaking.

"Oh, I guess just about everybody knows it now. She told a lot of people, and they told the rest. And she was always so smiling and pleasant to everyone—and so glad herself all the time! I guess they couldn't help knowing it. Now since she's been hurt, everybody feels so bad—especially because she feels bad because she can't find anything to be glad about. So they've been coming to tell her how glad she's made *them*—hoping that'll help. You see, she's always wanted everybody to play the game with her."

"Well, I know somebody who'll play it now," Miss Polly choked, as she ran up to Pollyanna's room.

"You've had another visitor today, my dear," announced Miss Polly, in a shaky voice. "Do you remember Mrs. Payson?"

"I sure do! She's awfully nice, and so is her husband. Only they don't seem to know how nice the other one is. Sometimes they fight. They're poor, too. But they don't ever get missionary barrels, because he isn't a missionary minister like . . ." Pollyanna stopped herself, blushing.

"Even so, she's got perfectly beautiful

rings," Pollyanna continued. "But she says she's got one ring too many, and that she's going to throw it away and get a divorce."

"But they aren't going to get a divorce, dear," Aunt Polly explained. "They're going to stay together right where they are."

"Oh, I'm so glad! Then they'll be there so I can go and see—Oh, dear!" the little girl broke off gloomily. "Aunt Polly, why can't I remember that my legs don't work anymore? And that I won't ever, ever again be able to go see Mrs. Payson and Mr. Pendleton and . . ."

"There, there," choked her aunt. "Perhaps you'll drive up sometime. But I haven't told you everything Mrs. Payson said. She wanted you to know that they're going to stay together and play the game—just as you wanted them to."

Pollyanna smiled through teary eyes. "Did they really? Oh, I *am* glad of that!"

"That's why she told you, Pollyanna. To make you *glad*."

Pollyanna looked up in surprise. "Why, Aunt Polly, you spoke as if you knew about the game. Do you?"

"Yes, dear. Nancy told me. I think it's a beautiful game. And from now on, I'm going to play it, too—with you."

"Oh, Aunt Polly! I'm so glad! You see, all along I've wanted you more than anybody else to play it with."

Aunt Polly struggled to steady her voice. "Yes, dear. Why, Pollyanna, I think the whole town is playing that game with you—even the minister! When I saw Mr. Ford this morning, he had a message for you. He said he hasn't stopped being glad about those 800 rejoicing verses you told him about. Now everyone is playing the game. And the whole town is wonderfully happier. And all because of one little girl who taught them how to be glad!"

Pollyanna clapped her hands. "Oh, I'm so glad!" she exclaimed. Then suddenly her face lit up. "Why, Aunt Polly! There is something I can be glad about! I can be glad I've *had* my legs! Otherwise, I could never have done that!"

Chapter
29

Through an Open Window

One by one the short winter days came and went. For Pollyanna, though, they were long and sometimes full of pain. But she was determined to turn a cheerful face toward whatever came. She felt she really needed to play the game, now that Aunt Polly was playing it, too. And Aunt Polly managed to find so many things to be glad about!

Like Mrs. Snow, Pollyanna was knitting wonderful things out of brightly colored yarns. And, also like Mrs. Snow, knitting made Pollyanna glad she at least had her hands and arms.

Occasionally Pollyanna saw people. And always there were loving messages from the people she could not see. Each one brought her something new to think about.

Once she saw John Pendleton, who told her how well Jimmy Bean was doing and what a fine boy he was becoming. Twice she saw Jimmy Bean, who told her what a great home he had and how Mr. Pendleton was a super "family." Both said it was all because of her.

"Which makes me that much gladder that I've *had* my legs," Pollyanna later confided to her aunt.

The winter passed, and spring came. Pollyanna did everything that Dr. Mead had prescribed. But there was no change in her condition. It seemed, indeed, that Pollyanna would never walk again.

Everyone in Beldingsville kept informed about Pollyanna. But one man in particular worried more than the rest. When things did not get better, his distress turned into despair—as well as determination. One Saturday morning, the determination finally won out. That's when Dr. Thomas Chilton made up his mind to pay a visit to Mr. John Pendleton.

"Pendleton," the doctor began, abruptly, "I've come to you because you know more than anyone else about my relationship with Miss Polly Harrington."

"Yes," John Pendleton answered, trying not to sound surprised and curious. In fact, he did know that Polly Harrington and Thomas Chilton had once been in love.

"Pendleton, I want to see that child. I want to examine her. I *must* examine her."

"Well, why can't you?"

"Why *can't* I! Pendleton, you know very well that I haven't been inside that house for more than fifteen years. Here's what you don't know. Miss Polly Harrington told me that if she ever again asked me inside, it meant she had changed her mind and would marry me. I sure don't see her asking me in now."

"But couldn't you go without being asked? Couldn't you swallow your pride and forget the quarrel—?"

"Forget the quarrel!" the doctor interrupted. "Why, I'd go there on my knees if it would do any good. I'm concerned about professional— not personal—issues. I can't just go in and treat another doctor's patient!"

"Chilton, what was the quarrel about anyway?"

"Oh, the same as any lovers' quarrel," the doctor said angrily, as he stormed over to the window. "Nothing at all—compared to the years of misery that followed it. Forget about the quarrel! Pendleton, I must see that child. It may mean life or death. Pendleton, I honestly believe there's a good chance that Pollyanna Whittier could walk again!"

Jimmy Bean just happened to be sitting under that very window. He was doing his Saturday morning chore of pulling up weeds. At this, his ears opened wide.

"Walk!" John Pendleton exclaimed. "What do you mean?"

"I mean that her case sounds very much like one that a college friend of mine has just helped. He specializes in this sort of thing—and has been writing me about his work. But I won't know unless I see the girl myself!"

John Pendleton exclaimed, "You must see her, man! Couldn't you arrange to do so through Dr. Warren?"

The doctor shook his head. "I'm afraid not. Warren's been very decent, though. He suggested that Miss Harrington consult with me. But she refused so strongly that he didn't dare ask her again. But Pendleton, I've got to see that child! Think what it might mean to her if I did!"

"And think what it will mean if you don't!"

"But how can I see her unless her aunt requests it? She's too proud and too angry to ask me. Especially after what she said it would mean if she did. Just think! The only things keeping Pollyanna from walking again are foolish pride and professional etiquette!"

"But if she could be made to understand . . ." suggested John Pendleton.

"And who's going to do that?" demanded the doctor bitterly.

"I don't know. I don't know," John Pendleton groaned.

Outside the window, Jimmy Bean whispered, joyously, "By golly, I know who!"

So he crept around the corner of the house, and then ran with all his might down Pendleton Hill.

Chapter 30

Jimmy Takes Control

"It's Jimmy Bean," Nancy announced. "He wants to see you, ma'am."

"Me?" Miss Polly asked, quite surprised. "Are you sure he doesn't mean Miss Pollyanna? He may see her a few minutes today if he likes."

"Yes'm. I told him. But he said it was you he wanted."

"Very well," Miss Polly said wearily.

Breathlessly, Jimmy Bean started speaking. "Ma'am, I guess what I'm doing is awful. But it's for Pollyanna. And for her I'd walk over hot coals or face you or—or anything. And I think you would, too, if you thought there was a chance for her to walk again. So I came here to tell you it's only pride and professional—*something* that's keeping Pollyanna from walking. I knew if you understood, you'd ask Dr. Chilton to come here and . . ."

"What!" Miss Polly interrupted, her surprise turning to anger.

Jimmy sighed. "I didn't want to make you mad. That's why I started by telling you about her walking again."

"Jimmy, what are you talking about?"

Jimmy took a deep breath. "Well, Dr. Chilton came to see Mr. Pendleton. The window was open, and I heard them talk."

"You listened in on a private conversation!"

"Well, I wasn't trying to! Anyway, I'm glad I listened. And you will be, too. Why, it may help Pollyanna walk again!"

"Jimmy, what do you mean?" Now Miss Polly leaned forward eagerly.

"Well, Dr. Chilton knows some doctor somewhere who can cure Pollyanna. But he can't tell for sure until he sees her. And he wants so badly to see her. But he told Mr. Pendleton that you wouldn't let him."

Miss Polly blushed deeply. "But Jimmy, I can't! I couldn't! That is, I didn't know!"

"That's why I came to tell you. So you *would* know! They said that you told Dr. Warren you wouldn't let Dr. Chilton come. And Dr. Chilton couldn't come unless you asked him because of pride and professional—something. And they wished somebody could make you understand. Only they didn't know who could. So that's why I came. And did I make you understand?"

"Yes, Jimmy. But who is the doctor? Are they *sure* he could make Pollyanna walk?"

"It's somebody Dr. Chilton knows. And he's just cured somebody that Dr. Chilton thinks is just like Pollyanna. So you'll let him come, won't you? Now that you understand?"

Miss Polly turned her head from side to side. After a minute, she said in a shaky voice, "Yes. I'll let Dr. Chilton see her. Now run home quickly, Jimmy! I've got to speak to Dr. Warren and ask him to call in Dr. Chilton right away!"

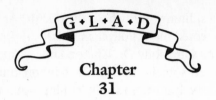

A New Uncle

That afternoon, Pollyanna lay in bed, watching the dancing colors on the ceiling. When she turned to see Dr. Warren enter the room, she noticed a tall, kind-eyed man following close behind.

"Dr. Chilton! Oh, Dr. Chilton! How glad I am to see you!" Pollyanna exclaimed joyously. "But of course, if Aunt Polly doesn't want . . ."

"It's all right, my dear. Don't worry," Miss Polly reassured her. "I told Dr. Chilton that I wanted him to look you over—with Dr. Warren—today."

"Oh, then you asked him to come," Pollyanna murmured happily.

"Yes, dear. I asked him. That is . . ." But it was too late. Miss Polly saw the look of happiness that suddenly appeared on Dr. Chilton's face. Blushing deeply, she hurried out of the room.

Dr. Chilton took both of Pollyanna's hands. "Little girl, I think today you did one of the very gladdest jobs you've ever done."

That evening, a wonderfully different Aunt Polly sat down beside Pollyanna. There was no one else in the room.

"Pollyanna, dear, I want you to be the first to know. Some day I'm going to let Dr. Chilton be your uncle. And it's you that did it all! Oh, Pollyanna, I'm so happy! And so glad! Darling!"

Pollyanna clapped her hands. "Oh, Aunt Polly! Were you the loving person's hand and heart he wanted so long ago? You were! I know you were! And that's what he meant by saying I'd done the gladdest job of all today. I'm so glad! Why, Aunt Polly, I'm so glad that I don't even mind my legs anymore!"

Aunt Polly swallowed a sob. "Perhaps some day, dear . . ."Aunt Polly stopped. She didn't dare tell her yet about the great hope that Dr. Chilton had put into her heart. But Pollyanna thought what she did say was wonderful enough.

"Next week, Pollyanna," she explained, "you're going to take a journey. You'll be carried on cars and carriages to a great doctor many miles from here. He has a big house where he works with people just like you. He's a dear friend of Dr. Chilton's. And we're going to see what he can do for you!"

Chapter
32

Which Is a Letter from Pollyanna

Dear Aunt Polly and Uncle Tom,

Oh, I *can!* I can! I can *walk!* I did today—all the way from my bed to the window. It was six steps. How good it was to be on legs again!

All the doctors stood around and smiled. And all the nurses stood beside them and cried. But I don't see why they cried. I wanted to sing and shout and yell! Oh, just think! I can walk, walk, *walk!*

Now I don't mind that I've been here almost ten months. And I'm still so glad, Aunt Polly, that you came here and got married right beside my bed—just so I could see you. You always do think of the gladdest things!

Pretty soon, they say, I'll be going

home. I wish I could walk all the way there. I really do! I don't think I'll ever want to ride anywhere anymore. It will be so good just to walk!

You know, I'm glad now that I lost my legs for a while. For you never, never know how perfectly lovely legs are until you don't have them to use.

Tomorrow I'm going to walk eight steps!

With heaps of love to everybody,

Pollyanna

About the Author

$\mathcal{E}$leanor Hodgman Porter was born on December 19, 1868, in Littleton, New Hampshire. She studied for several years at the New England Conservatory of Music. She then began her career as a singer, performing in concerts and in churches. In 1892, Eleanor Hodgman married John Lyman Porter, a Vermont businessman, and moved to Massachusetts. There she gave up her singing career and began writing short stories for magazines. She published her first short story in 1901, and her first full-length novel in 1907. Beginning with *Pollyanna*, Porter wrote at least one book every year for the rest of her life. In all, she published 16 novels and several collections of short stories.

Porter is best known for her beloved character, Pollyanna Whittier. *Pollyanna* was first published in 1913. The book became an instant success. In fact, the publisher had trouble printing enough copies to keep up with the demand. In its first year, so many people bought the book that *Pollyanna* ranked 8th on the best-seller list. The next year it was the second most popular book in the country among both children and adults. No one knows exactly how many copies of *Pollyanna* have been sold since 1913, because it has been published in many different languages all over the world.

Then as now, readers were delighted and inspired by Pollyanna's positive attitude in the face of difficulty. All over the country, both adults and children formed "Glad Clubs." The public demanded a second book about Pollyanna, which Porter wrote two years later. In *Pollyanna Grows Up*, the only sequel that Porter herself wrote, Pollyanna travels to Europe, where she faces new challenges as a young adult.

But *Pollyanna's* popularity has not been limited only to books. In 1916, the famous stage actress Helen Hayes starred in a Broadway play based on Porter's novel. A few years later, the popular silent film star Mary Pickford played the role of Pollyanna in a movie adaptation. In 1960, Disney produced a film version starring Hayley Mills. And in 2004, PBS created a "Masterpiece Theatre" production for television.

On May 21, 1920, Eleanor Hodgman Porter died from tuberculosis at the age of 51. But the character she created and her message about optimism continue to encourage and guide readers. Four other writers have published a total of 10 different sequels to *Pollyanna*. Many other people have written stories based on this engaging character. You can even find the word "Pollyanna" in the dictionary!

And in 2002, Porter's hometown of Littleton, New Hampshire placed a brand-new statue in front of the public library. Unlike many public monuments, though, this statue does not pay tribute to a military leader or a famous politician. Instead, it honors a hero of a different kind—one who inspires us to face challenges with grace and optimism. For this local hero is a little girl named Pollyanna.

About the Book

It has been said that one should never underestimate the power of positive thinking. But can a positive attitude really bring about important and lasting change?

Pollyanna shows that one little girl's positive approach to life helps many people find happiness, courage, beauty, and meaning in their own lives. By seeing and appreciating what is good, Pollyanna brings out the best in herself and others. By teaching others to play the "glad game," Pollyanna shows how anyone can learn to face disappointment with optimism. Pollyanna's positive attitude has the power to change not only herself and her friends. In the end, it transforms an entire town.

Pollyanna brightens her world by focusing on what she has, rather than on what she lacks. When she first comes to live with her Aunt Polly, she moves into a dreary room without rugs or pictures. But instead of being defeated by her disappointment, she notices the lovely view from the window. As she tells Nancy, "Who needs pictures with a view like that? Oh, now I'm really glad she let me have this room!"

Indeed, Pollyanna has the power to bring out the beauty in everything—and everyone. Pollyanna brings color to Mrs. Snow's room—and her life— by opening her curtains and hanging prisms in the windows. She points out Mrs. Snow's "big and dark" eyes, and her "curly black hair." After arranging Mrs. Snow's hair, Pollyanna insists that Mrs. Snow look at herself in the mirror. And for the first time since her illness, Mrs. Snow begins to appreciate herself and her life.

Pollyanna's belief in the goodness of others brings out the best in them. Unlike most people in town, Pollyanna accepts Mrs. Payson and focuses on her good qualities. The little girl's nonjudgmental kindness and trust inspire the Paysons to stay together instead of getting a divorce. Pollyanna's optimism also helps Mrs. Tarbell cope with the loss of her daughter.

And Pollyanna's gentle encouragement finally convinces Widow Benton, "the saddest woman in town," to bring color back into her life.

Pollyanna's faith in the kindness of others strengthens her hope and determination. Because she expects a positive response, Pollyanna is able to face the Ladies' Aid Society without fear. And it is Pollyanna's steadfast optimism that eventually brings out John Pendleton's inner kindness and his faith in Jimmy Bean. Pollyanna never doubts that her Aunt Polly really is a "good and kind" person. Although Aunt Polly tries to resist, Pollyanna's patience and faith in her aunt's love ultimately open up the lonely woman's heart.

By focusing on what people can do, Pollyanna also brings meaning and usefulness to their lives. Pollyanna helps Mrs. Snow realize that she can at least use her arms and hands. As Mrs. Snow stops feeling sorry for herself, she starts thinking about other people's needs, and begins knitting blankets for babies in hospitals. Instead of complaining about what she doesn't have, Mrs. Snow learns to share what she does have with others.

Pollyanna's positive spirit helps other people heal—both physically and emotionally. Dr. Chilton even wishes he could "prescribe her, the way I'd prescribe pills." After the accident when he broke his leg, John Pendleton is too angry to try to get better. When she first visits him,